THE A-TEAM V:
TEN PERCENT OF TROUBLE

A grotesque, scaly hand lighted on Mickey's shoulders and a broad, ominous shadow fell across the ground before him. Mickey turned to see a monstrous apparition hovering before him, covered with more scales and dragging behind it a long tail as thick as a full-bellied python. The monster had two heads. It was the second head that talked, asking Mickey, 'Take a picture with Aqua Maniac? Glub-glub, scream-scream?'

'Thanks, but we don't have a camera, pal,' said Mickey. 'Why don't you go ooze over someone else?'

'Then how about just taking a ride?' the Aqua Maniac asked. 'That is, if you're still interested in hiring the A-Team.'

'The A-Team?' Mickey gasped.

'Hannibal Smith,' the Aqua Maniac introduced himself, offering his claws for a handshake. 'At your service.'

Also available

THE A-TEAM V:
TEN PERCENT OF TROUBLE

A novel by Charles Heath

Based on the television series 'The A-Team'
Created by Frank Lupo and Stephen J. Cannell
Adapted from the episodes 'Steel' written by
Frank Lupo, and 'Maltese Cow' written by
Thomas Szollosi & Richard Christian Matheson

TARGET

A TARGET BOOK

published by
the Paperback Division of
W.H. ALLEN & Co. PLC

A Target Book
Published in 1984
by the Paperback Division of
W.H. Allen & Co. PLC
44 Hill Street, London W1X 8LB

Printed in Great Britain by
Anchor Brendon Ltd, Tiptree, Essex

ISBN 0 426 198441

PROLOGUE

It was the first week after the clocks had been turned back for Daylight Savings. The sunrise came an hour earlier, but so did dusk. It was only a little after five when the sun dropped through a bank of clouds crouched over the Pacific and turned the colour of blood before dipping beneath the horizon and leaving the sky tainted with shades of red. A crisp nip of autumn chill rode on the offshore breeze, which blew all the way inland to the heart of the city, where work crews wrapped up their dayshifts against the approach of night. The sounds of jack-hammers, rivet guns, and mechanical cranes dwindled and men began descending from frameworks of steel girders and the brick shells of buildings being erected or destroyed. Near the corner of Federal and Denomville, a handful of workers put away their tools and headed off to their cars, leaving behind the half-demolished warehouse they had been labouring over for the past few weeks. While they drove off to their respective suppers and stints before the television set, two crew members stayed behind.

Mickey Stern looked like the retired pro linebacker he was. Although in his mid-fifties, he'd kept his weight in check and cut an imposing figure in his coveralls and flannel shirt. He wore a Dodger ball cap over his greying hair, and he had a habit of fingering his neatly trimmed beard whenever he was nervous. Tonight he looked like he was on the verge of plucking the beard from his face,

5

hair by hair, as he paced across the littered sidewalk to the weathered Airstream trailer that served as his office and part-time home.

Mickey's niece, Randy, had brought the news that was causing him so much consternation. She was dressed in jeans and a sweatshirt, but there was a graceful beauty about her that seemed more suited to cocktail dresses or designer clothes. She walked alongside her uncle, cringing at the transformation that had come over him in the past few seconds. She didn't like to see him like this, because she knew the toll his temper was capable of taking on him.

'Please, Uncle Mickey. Try not to get so upset.'

'Not get upset!?' Mickey railed, pounding a fist into his calloused palm. 'What does Gunderson want from me, for crying out loud? Blood? Who is he anyway?'

'I told you, he's the new guy at the City Planning Commission,' Randy said, waiting outside the trailer while her uncle went in to grab a couple of sodas from the mini-refrigerator. 'I think they just want the work finished. It's pretty obvious.'

'If I could get the next payment, I might be able to *do* that!' Mickey groused as he handed Randy one of the cans and pulled the top off the other. 'Maybe I should talk to him instead of you.'

They walked away from the trailer and sat down on a stack of lumber next to the crane with the wrecking ball. 'I really don't think that's wise,' Randy said. She took a long sip of her root beer, then wiped a fleck of foam from her upper lip before continuing. 'Look, the contract they signed when we took the bid was for four payments. They've already advanced us the second when they didn't have to. There's just no way we can get them to pay again when we're this far behind schedule. We haven't even finished getting the steel down yet.'

Mickey looked at the web of girders rising before him. Framed against the darkening hues of sunset, they seemed almost like remnants from a long-decayed civilization, unearthed ruins holding untold secrets of forgotten rituals and customs. To Mickey, though, they represented the means for his livelihood, elusive means that took on a taunting aspect by the mere virtue of remaining aloft after all these days. 'They know I've had setbacks,' he muttered, stroking his beard again. 'I'm short-handed on labour besides everything else that's gone wrong around here.'

'But that's not Mr Gunderson's fault.'

'Of course it isn't! It's Denham's fault, that chiselling slime!' Seething with fury, Mickey drained his soda and crushed the can in his palm, then hurled it into the trash dumpster several yards away. 'He's the one who's been sabotaging me! All I gotta do is get another strike against me and the contract'll end up in his lap. He oughta get the chair! Damn it, just thinking about that no-good makes me want to. . .'

The man's voice trailed off and he winced as he put a hand to his chest.

'Uncle Mickey? What's the matter?'

'Nothin',' he mumbled, massaging the spot between his shirt pockets. 'It's nothin'. . .'

'Don't give me that,' Randy snapped. She reached for her uncle's pocket and pulled out a small bottle filled with white pills. She tapped one out and handed it to Mickey. 'You know what the doctor said about those pains. You're supposed to take the nitro every time you feel them. Your health's nothing to risk by playing macho games. Now take this!'

Mickey make a face and set the tablet under his tongue, letting it dissolve into his system. The pain in his chest subsided and he pulled his hand away. He noticed the look of anxiety stamped on his niece's face and forced a smile. 'Hey, knock it off, willya? It's just a little angina. Musta been that sandwich I had for lunch.'

'Uncle Mickey. . .'

'I mean it,' Mickey chuckled. 'Always feeding me that junk from those health food stores you shop at. It's not Denham or heart attacks that'll do me in. More likely it'll be whole grain bread and bean sprouts.'

Randy put a hand on her uncle's shoulder and searched

his eyes, trying to peer past his facade of sudden good cheer. 'Please, Uncle, I love you too much to see you pushing yourself any harder than you have to. You know, maybe we should just let Denham have his way. Sure, we'd take a loss on this project, but there's still –'

'No way,' Mickey countered firmly. 'Sterns aren't quitters. Never were and they never will be if I have any say in the matter. I'm gonna see this job through, and I'm gonna get my company back to the point where I can pay some fool to work outta that trailer instead of me and I can set up shop in one of those fancy high-rises I worked up a sweat building all these years I've been in this crazy game.'

'That's what I keep trying to tell you,' Randy said. 'It's not a game. And you aren't in the kind of shape to be going tooth-and-nail trying to prove something that doesn't need proving. Start thinking of enjoying yourself. You've earned that right. You owe it to yourself.'

Mickey reached up and clasped his hand over Randy's, then pulled it gently off his shoulder. He kissed his niece's fingers as he rose to his feet. 'You sound just like your aunt, Randy. Always wantin' to put me in a rocker with a jack-knife and a big enough stick to whittle away the rest of my years. I know you mean well, love, but you just don't know how this old geezer ticks.' Standing up, Mickey gestured to the equipment of his trade and the framework of the building he was in charge of razing. 'This is my life. This is what I enjoy, even if it sounds like I'm bitching every inch of the way. It's in my blood. You can't take it out of me.'

'You're wrong, Uncle Mickey,' Randy argued. 'I'm telling you, you're wrong. There's so much more that you –'

Randy's words were drowned out by a sudden explosion. Somewhere inside the old Airstream, something blew up with so much force that the entire shell of the trailer ruptured like a dropped egg. Flames surged out into the night air as flying debris showered the work site. Mickey reflexively moved between the trailer and Randy, tackling his niece to the ground as a blazing shard of wood shot

8

past them. Two more explosions, smaller than the first, rocked the trailer off its foundation. The Airstream toppled to one side, and the flames crept higher as more of the contents ignited.

Mickey rolled away from his niece, grimacing with pain as he clutched at his chest. 'Damn. . .'

'Uncle Mickey!'

Randy quickly crawled over to her uncle's side and held him down as she got out one of his pills and gave it to him. He took it reluctantly as he craned his neck to catch a glimpse of the burning trailer. 'Damn,' he muttered again.

'You stay put,' Randy insisted, cradling Mickey's head in her lap and running her fingers across his perspiring brow. 'Never mind anything else, just stay put!'

'Never mind anything else!?' Mickey howled mockingly. 'He bombed my trailer! That bastard bombed my trailer!'

'You don't know that, Uncle.'

'Oh, right, I suppose you're going to tell me it was an accident!'

A voice in the darkness called out. 'Then again, maybe you just got careless, Stern.'

Both Mickey and Randy looked in the direction the voice had come from. Three men emerged from the shadows next to the large crane. The man in the middle was Carl Denham, a lean, dark man with a lopsided smile sliced across his narrow face. His brown eyes were like gun bores, trained on his long-time adversary. On either side of him were two hulks with physiques similar to Mickey Stern in his football prime, although they looked more accustomed to throwing punches than passes.

'How dare you!' Randy hissed at the three men.

Denham ignored the woman and continued to stare at Mickey. 'Word's out this isn't a safe place to be working, Stern.'

Mickey's medication had calmed his heart but not his temper. Pushing aside his niece's arm, he sat up and pointed at the burning rubble that had once been his trailer. 'Damn it, my payroll was in there!'

Denham clucked his tongue with false pity. 'Gee, that's

too bad, pal. Rough break.'

Mickey struggled to his feet. Randy tried to hold him back as Denham's goons stepped forward to block the way. Mickey realised the futility of trying to get past them and contented himself with wagging a fist at Denham as he vowed, 'You won't stop me this easy, you hear me, Denham!? You just wrote yourself a ticket to the state pen, and I'm gonna see to it that it gets cashed in!'

'I don't think so, Mick ol' boy.' Denham paused to light a cigarette, then blew a plume of smoke between his men and into Mickey's face. 'You're outta business, Stern. This time it was just your payroll. Next time. . . who knows? Maybe you and your niece are in the wrong place at the wrong time. . . know what I'm saying?'

The smoke stung Mickey's eyes and wound its way up his nostrils, but he refused to show any sign of discomfort. He met Denham's gaze and held it with his own, saying nothing. The two men continued to face off for some time, surrounded by the sound of flame and the distant wail of a fire engine. Then Denham turned around and walked with his two men back into the shadows.

'Nobody threatens Mickey Stern and gets away with it!' Mickey shouted defiantly. 'Nobody!'

There was no answer from Denham, save for the sound of car doors opening, then closing. An engine growled into life and Denham's car shot out onto the main road, several seconds before the first police car arrived on the scene.

'It's over, Uncle Mickey,' Randy whispered, taking the man's hand and clenching it tight. 'He's not going to stop at anything to get his way.'

'Neither am I,' Mickey vowed. 'Neither am I.'

'You can't stand up to him alone,' Randy told him. 'And you know you're not going to risk the lives of the men who work for you. We don't have a choice, Uncle Mickey. Let's get out while we still can.'

Mickey stood firm, staring at the trailer. The two police officers piled out of their cruiser and came over. One of them asked, 'What happened here?'

Without taking his eyes of the Airstream, Mickey calmly replied, 'Somebody just forced my hand, that's all. . .'

ONE

The large pond was still and tranquil. The plump clouds reflected on its surface looked like dumplings in a great bowl of soup. And then a grey blur rushed through the depths, raising ripples with the fury of its motion. The blur took shape in a matter of seconds as it skimmed beneath the water. A single, triangular fin broke the surface and sliced the water like a dull knife as it followed an unerring course toward a slow-moving tram that was rolling past the edge of the pond, filled with unsuspecting tourists. A child amidst the group happened to spot the fin, and she pointed it out to the others as she screamed, 'Mommy, it's Jaws!'

Even as the others turned to look, the wide, blunt snout of the shark parted the waters and exposed the rows of white jagged teeth that gave the creature its unsavoury reputation. Many of the tourists instinctively recoiled from the attack, some of them overpowering the girl's screams with their own. Others, however, only laughed as they raised their cameras and clicked off pictures of the would-be flesh-eater which snapped its massive jaws far from harm's way and followed alongside the tram with the unthreatening persistence of a beggar soliciting alms. The more the shark remained halfway out of the water, the less intimidating it became. The rubbery quiver of the teeth, the synthetic sheen of its skin, the mechanical clicking of the rollers that carried the beast along its underwater track – these and other tell-tale signs cracked the illusion of terror and allowed even the most gullible of passengers to realise that the shark posed no more threat than a costumed trick-or-treater at Halloween.

In the back of the tram, a uniformed tour guide raised a microphone to his lips and assured his charges, 'Don't worry, ladies and gentlemen, we're told that Bruce the Shark was fed just a few hours ago, so he's probably just looking for a little heavy-duty floss.' As he waited for chuckles that never came, the guide leaned out of the tram. He looked like he was about to stick his head in the shark's mouth, but at the last second he pulled away, making an anguished face as he groaned, 'Anybody out there got a little breath-freshener while we're at it?'

Randy and Mickey were riding in the tram, a few rows away from the guide. Mickey rolled his eyes while his niece watched the shark slip back beneath the waters of the pond. 'I'd hate to meet up with the real thing,' she reflected.

'I don't think we have to worry about it,' Mickey said.

As the tram headed away from the pond, the guide continued his well-rehearsed patter. 'Bruce's last job was working on 'Jaws 3-D', but now he's looking to break out of typecasting and land a role in an upcoming gangster film. It's basically a love story about a soft-hearted loan shark. It's called 'Okay, One More Week 3-D.'

It was the tourists' turn to groan. Mickey crossed his arms and shook his head. When he had his niece's attention, he muttered, 'You're worried about me getting a heart attack and you bring me here? Sheesh, what next? I mean, first we spend hours standing on street corners in the middle of the night, then we have to put up with some fortune cookie yoyo in a Chinese laundry and a wino who lives in the alley behind the Ivar Theatre. And now it's sharks and frustrated comedians torturing us with bad jokes. . .'

'I told you not to come,' Randy reminded him. 'I said I'd handle it all myself.'

'Hey, since when do you tell me things?' Mickey

14

snapped gruffly. 'I'm your uncle. You don't tell me what to do.'

'Nobody tells you what to do,' Randy said with a smile, trying to diffuse her uncle's temper before it could get the better of him.

'Damn right!' Mickey noticed a man across the aisle training his camera on Randy and shouted at him, 'And what do you think you're doin', huh?'

The other man snapped off a quick picture, then flashed Randy a grin before turning his attention to the simulated parting of the Red Sea, taking place at the head of the tram.

'Take it easy, Uncle Mickey, would you?'

'All these jerks lookin' at you like that,' Mickey grumbled, eyeing Randy's shorts and halter. 'What do you have to dress like that for, anyway?'

Randy snickered, 'So those jerks will look at me like that.'

As his niece traded flirting glances with yet another tourist, Mickey rolled his eyes again. 'Look, did we come here looking for help or are you just trying to fill out your social calendar?'

'I'm just keeping an eye open for the man we're supposed to meet,' Randy replied lamely.

'Don't you remember what Mr Lee said?' Mickey countered. 'We're not supposed to find them, they'll find us. Typical Hollywood line.'

After passing through the Red Sea, the tram rolled into an area surrounded by souvenir shops, food stands, and props and vehicles from various Universal blockbusters. There were also a few employees wearing costumes of famous and not-so-famous characters, mingling around as they waited for the inevitable request to have their pictures taken alongside sightseers who figured this was the closest they'd come to rubbing elbows with the stars.

'We're going to take a ten minute break,' the tram guide announced to his minions as he hopped down to the ground. 'You'll find refreshment stands and rest rooms here, along with shops that sell film, for those fledgling paparazzi among you.'

Picking up his cue, a Keystone Kop wandered up to the tram guide and waved a nightstick in his face. 'Who are you calling a fledgling paparazzi? Don't you know this is a family facility? I oughta run you in for using words like that.'

As Mickey followed his niece out of the tram, he told the two employees, 'Somebody oughta run the both of you in for using jokes like that.'

The man who had taken Randy's picture moments before raised his camera for another shot, and Randy turned coyly, smiling back at him over her shoulder. Mickey grabbed the crook of her arm and led her away.

'Maybe that's the guy we're looking for,' Randy protested.

'No way,' Mickey said. 'After all the footwork we've done to get this far, I'm expecting somebody with a little more class.'

Just then a grotesque, scaly hand lighted on Mickey's shoulders and a broad, ominous shadow fell across the ground before him. Mickey turned to see a monstrous apparition hovering before him, covered with more scales and dragging behind it a long tail as thick as a full-bellied python. The monster had two heads. One rose high in the air, looking like something that got its genes from a giraffe and the Creature from the Black Lagoon. The other head was half-concealed in the abomination's throat so that there was a face where the Adam's apple might have otherwise been. It was the second head that talked, asking Mickey, 'Take a picture with Aqua Maniac? Glub-glub, scream-scream?'

Mickey stared down the creature as if it were something conjured up in his mind by a bad case of indigestion. 'Thanks, but we don't have a camera, pal. Why don't you go ooze over someone else?'

'Then how about just taking a ride?' the Aqua Maniac asked. Noting Mickey's hesitation, he added, 'That is, if you're still interested in hiring the A-Team.'

'The A-Team?' Randy gasped. She couldn't have been

more astounded if the Aqua Maniac had claimed to be the secret identity taken up by Jimmy Hoffa after his mysterious disappearance years before.

'Hannibal Smith,' the Aqua Maniac introduced himself, offering his claws for a handshake. 'At your service.'

'I don't believe it,' Mickey said. 'You gotta be kiddin'. This can't be real.'

'This is real as it gets,' Hannibal informed him. Pointing past Mickey's shoulder, he said, 'Head over to that tram with the VIP sticker on it. I'll try to keep up with you, but my tail has a tendency to slow me down.'

As Mickey led Randy across the grounds, he leaned close to her and whispered, 'I gotta have my head examined for following through on this.'

'They have a reputation for being eccentric, but that doesn't mean they can't do the job,' Randy said. 'It's still our best chance.'

'Then heaven help us.'

Hannibal waddled as fast as he could inside the costume, but the Aqua Maniac was not built for speed. Before he'd taken half a dozen steps, he was besieged by a pair of rambunctious children. The boy tried to tackle him, plowing into Hannibal's leg with all his wee might, while his sister picked up the tail as if she wanted to play jumprope with it.

'Johnny! Sarah!' the children's mother called out as she rushed over with her trusty Instamatic. 'Be nice to Mr Aqua Maniac or he won't let me take your picture with him.'

'That's right, kiddies,' Hannibal said, plucking young Sarah off his tail as if she were no more than a pesky flea. 'Mr Aqua Maniac eats bad boys and girls for breakfast, and he hasn't had a bite all morning. . .'

Johnny gave up trying to bring down Hannibal, and the three of them posed long enough for the children's mother to take their picture. Than Hannibal gave each of the kids a pat on the head and motioned for them to move away.

'No, I wanna stay with you forever!' Sarah wailed.

As the girl's mother came to Hannibal's rescue, he told

the child, 'I'd love to have you hang around, honey, but terrorizing metropolises is hard work. It'd cut into your nap time, and I can see you can't do without that.'

Once the kids were out of his way, Hannibal unzipped his costume enough to get at his cigars. Igniting a fragrant cheroot, he resumed the arduous trek to the tram where Mickey and Randy were headed. On the way, he passed by a fellow employee dressed up like Frankenstein.

'Cover for me, wouldya, Mel?' he asked. 'I'll be back in ten.'

Mel held out a green palm and Hannibal gave him five. 'Sure thing, you maniac you.'

'Ah, yes,' Hannibal snorted, blowing smoke out of his nose. 'There's no business like show business. . .'

TWO

Templeton Peck was sitting in the back of the VIP tram, wearing a custom-tailored leather jacket over his impeccably matched slacks and shirt. He lounged with an air of self-assurance, as if he were an idle billionaire who'd hired out the tram for his own personal tour of the studios to see if he might be interested in bankrolling his pet project under the Universal banner. B.A. Baracus, on the other hand, stood nearby with the glowering vigilance of a professional bodyguard. Thick, gleaming biceps protruded from his khaki vest, threatening to burst the gold armbands that comprised a mere fraction of the glitter he adorned himself with. His dark eyes scanned the crowd of tourists milling nearby and picked out the approaching figures of Mickey and Randy, followed by the hulking presence of Hannibal the Aqua Maniac.

'They're comin', Face,' he told Peck.

'Thanks, B.A.,' Peck responded drolly, 'I see them. Take the wheel.'

As B.A. climbed out of the tram and headed for the front of the vehicle, Peck stood up and waved the prospective clients aboard. Hannibal had considerable difficulty fitting into the tram, due to the added height of his second head, but he finally managed to squeeze in. Just as Mickey and Randy were settling into their seats, the same photographer who had been taking pictures of Randy all morning drifted over, shutter clicking on his camera. Peck blocked the steps leading up to the tram and held a hand out like a traffic guard.

'Sorry, friend, but this tram's only for parties with VIP passes.'

Oblivious to the warning, the camera buff nuzzled his face against the viewfinder and focused on Randy once again. Just as the young woman's features were crystallizing into a sharp image, the viewfinder was suddenly filled by a scowling countenance of a bearded black man with a narrow strip of hair running down the middle of his otherwise bald head. The man with the camera clicked off the shot he'd intended for Randy, then peered uncertainly over his viewfinder at the obstruction between him and his subject.

'You hard of hearin', sucker?' B.A. demanded.

The other man nodded feebly and offered an apologetic smile. His lips fluttered nervously, like twin worms doing aerobics. B.A. grabbed him by the front of the shirt and barked in his ear, 'Take a hike or else you're gonna eat that camera, fool!'

The message was loud and clear, and the man headed off in long strides. B.A. waited until he was sure they weren't going to be bothered again, then took the driver's seat of the tram and meshed gears until the mini-train was rolling away from the concession area. Artificial bull-rushes bordered the tram on the right, while a western set gathered dust on the other side. Peck sat down across from Randy, eyeing her with an interest every bit as ingratiating as that she'd received from the photographer.

'Been enjoying the tour?' he asked her, flashing his orthodontist's dream of a smile. 'My favourite part's where you go over the rickety bridge and they have that landslide –'

Put it back in your duffel bag, fella,' Mickey interrupted. 'She's immune to those kinda cheap come-ons.'

'Oh. . .' Peck drew the curtain on his smile and slouched back in his seat.

'No, I'm not,' Randy contradicted her uncle as she offered Peck a mild smirk, made all the more alluring by

20

the twinkle in her eyes.

'Oh.' Peck repeated. His smile came back out for an encore.

'Look, I don't know what we're doing here at all any more,'' Mickey said, cracking his knuckles with exasperation. 'It wasn't my idea to contact you guys –'

'It was mine,' Randy said, suddenly serious. 'I'd read about the A-Team in the paper and tracked down one of your clients. He put me in touch with Mr Lee at a laundromat. Have you talked with him yet?'

'We wouldn't be here if we hadn't, now would we?' Hannibal puffed on his cigar and fussed a few seconds with the Aqua Maniac headpiece until he was able to shift the weight on his shoulders. Once he was more comfortable, he resumed, 'Mr Lee said you're about to lose your most important construction contract due to a certain number of unnatural accidents on the building site.'

'Unnatural, hah!' Mickey scoffed.

Randy explained. 'We're being sabotaged by a competitor, Carl Denham.'

'I can speak for myself!' Mickey retorted. Levelling his gaze at Hannibal, he seethed, 'We're being sabotaged by Denham, a weaselly skunk with about –'

'Is that Denham of Denham Construction and Wrecking?' Peck cut in, whistling softly. 'Boy, you sure know how to pick enemies. They're one of the biggest outfits around this town, aren't they? City and country contracts all over the place, unless I'm mistaken.'

'The guy's a bum!' Mickey insisted, slamming an angry fist against the armrest next to him. 'He's never run a legit business. Hell, the only way he's cornered the market is by undercutting any bid the rest of us can afford to put up for jobs around town.'

'Sounds fair enough to me,' Peck conceded.

'Yeah? Well, the way he's able to underbid is that he uses materials that aren't up to specifications. I'm talking about the basics, too. Low-grade concrete and steel. You name it, he'll stoop to it if it means bucks.'

Randy could sense her uncle's increasing agitation and

placed her hand over his in a pre-arranged signal for him to calm down and let her do the talking. She told Peck and Hannibal, 'Last year, Denham had a bridge come down over in Montebello during the winter rains. It was a miracle no one was hurt. Not only did he bribe his way out of losing his licence over it, but he also wrangled a contract to rebuild the bridge for twice the price he got the first time!'

Peck stared over at another of the trams, which was leading tourists across the track bridge he'd mentioned earlier that was able to quaver and rattle on command to give the passengers a dose of adrenalin-thrills. 'Sounds like he could get a job here real easy. The studios like things that are easy to break down once they finish shooting.'

More to the point, Hannibal said, 'Suppose all you've said is true. That still doesn't explain why he's out to sabotage you. I mean, he's got plenty of work to keep him busy and line his pockets. Why's he so hot and bothered by a small independent trying to earn a living?'

'We've traded a few words over the years, but I think that's only part of it,' Mickey said, struggling to keep himself under control. He popped a nitro tablet under his tongue to keep his heart from getting the shakes. 'All I know is I was able to wrangle this contract by a fluke. The city re-zoned that area and wanted the warehouse torn down so they could throw up more office space for their bureaucrats. Denham actually put in a lower bid for the job, but through some screwup at his office it came in too late to be considered. I got the job and he went through the roof. I don't know, maybe it's just an ego thing with him and he can't stand not getting something he wanted. At any rate, he's been hassling me and my crew ever since we hit the site. And he's playing for keeps. I got men in the hospital because of a few 'accidents', and there's been a few night raids on the site where I lost tools and had some of my big equipment vandalized. I started spending all my time at a trailer there, so Denham decided to blow that up, along with my payroll for this week.'

Randy added, 'The insurance company is looking at us sideways. Even worse, we can barely keep our men working for us any more.

'And I can't blame 'em!' Mickey said. 'I only have until Wednesday to come up with their salaries or they're all gonna walk. That's if they don't do it sooner on account of everything that's happened.'

B.A. veered the tram past a group of loin-clothed barbarians lounging outside the Conan exhibition, then started heading back. He was close enough to the others to have overheard the conversation, and he interjected, 'Hey, man, if you can't get anyone to work for you, what do you expect us to do? Five of us can't yank down one building and put up another one.'

Mickey sighed, feeling the weight of futility bearing down upon him. 'I don't know,' he mumbled dismally.

'What you can do,' Randy told the A-Team, 'Is back Denham off.'

'Hey, I said I can talk for myself,' Mickey sparked. Summoning a reserve of indignation, he told Hannibal, 'What you can do is back Denham off.'

Peck smirked at Randy. 'Nice relationship you and your uncle have.'

Mickey ignored Peck's sarcasm and rested his case. 'The last thing I want is a bunch of guys feeding their families on Society Security. But they can't be on the bricks forever and they sure aren't gonna get hired by Denham. Anyone who's punched a card with me is a big zero over there.'

As B.A. circled around the Cylons guarding the way to the Battlestar Galactica experience, Hannibal and Peck gazed at one another silently, as if conferring by mental telepathy. Their features failed to betray their feelings on the matter, but apparently they were split as to whether or not to take on the job, because Hannibal turned to B.A. and said, 'What do you think, big guy?'

B.A. mulled it over as he completed their round trip and brought the tram to a halt back at the concession area. 'I think I wanna meet this dude,' he finally said. 'Maybe help him with some of his bridgework . . . like busting up his mouth.'

Peck chuckled, 'Hey, B.A., that's pretty funny. You're developing a sense of humour.' When B.A. whirled around in his seat and glared, Peck stopped laughing. 'Slowly, but it is developing.'

Hannibal was the first one out of the tram. Putting his Aqua Maniac head back in its proper position, he stomped out his cigar with his monster feet as he informed Mickey and Randy, 'You've hired the A-Team. We'll get into our rates once we've had a chance to check out the worksite and figure out what we're up against. Fair enough?'

Randy looked to her uncle, who shrugged his shoulders as they disembarked from the tram. He said, 'We gotta do something. Okay, fair enough.'

'Good. Enjoy the rest of the tour.' Hannibal turned to his partners. 'Face, you spring Murdock and then'll we'll all regroup right after I finish my shift. Until then, as they say, the show must go on.'

As Hannibal shuffled his way back into the throng of tourists, Mickey and Randy watched him uncertainly.

'I hope we're doing the right thing,' Randy said.

'Me too.' Mickey stroked his beard as he stared at the bobbing tail of the Aqua Maniac. 'And I thought the guy in the Chinese laundry was weird. . .'

THREE

They were used to disturbances in Howling Mad Murdock's room at the Veteran's Hospital. His wide array of psychological disorders made him a living, breathing textbook study for the various interns and resident psychiatrists working at the facility. He was the only patient living on the west coast for whom a specific mental ailment was being named. Barring any unforeseen improvement in his condition, by the year's end the medical journals would witness the first mention of The Murdock Syndrome, so named after Howling Mad's incredible susceptibility to any number of disorders, ranging from psychotic hallucinations to paranoid delusion.

Today Murdock was in fine form.

As the afternoon shift was settling into its duties, a nurse and orderly stopped by Murdock's room to see how he was doing. One step into the room, the orderly froze with shock at the sound of an intense growling from the vicinity of Murdock's bed. Without bothering to risk a closer look, the orderly retreated to the hallway, shouting, 'Hey . . . hey! Back! Stay away!'

'What's going on?' the nurse gasped as she found herself being nudged away from the door.

'I don't know, man, but that sure as hell didn't sound like his dog Billy,' the orderly insisted. 'He's graduated to wolves, if you ask me.'

The nurse glanced over Murdock's chart and shook her head knowingly. 'The morning shift says he started working up to this after breakfast. It says something here about him finding a bone in his steak. That must have started it.'

'Yeah?' The orderly rolled up his sleeves like someone getting ready for a street brawl. 'Well, I for one have had it with that fraud. I say we dose him with some sodium pentathol and ship him out to the nearest pound and see if he still wants to carry on like he's Cujo's cousin.'

As the orderly re-entered the room with a loaded syringe, Peck hustled down the corridor toward the nurse, toting a black satchel that had gone out of style the same time as house calls and bedside manners. He wore a look of urgency, as if the fate of mankind, or at least the immediate vicinity, depended upon his presence.

'I'm looking for a Mr Murdock,' he told the nurse.

Inside Murdock's room, a raucous howl sounded, rattling the door with its intensity. It was followed by the frightened pleadings of the orderly. 'N-n-n-nice Murdock. Good boy. Sit!'

'I guess this must be the place,' Peck said, as if he hadn't graced these same halls a dozen times before in various disguises and under various pretexts for the same reason as he was here today.

'He started up earlier this morning,' the nurse explained to Peck. 'We're used to this sort of behaviour from Mr Murdock, but from the sound of it, he's got much worse. If I didn't know better I'd think he really had been bitten and contracted rabies. . .'

'Believe it.'

'But that's not possible,' the nurse claimed. 'His dog is a figment of his imagination.'

Another series of barks emanated from within the room.

'Some figment,' Peck said dubiously.

'I'm sorry, doctor, but I don't believe I know you and I don't think you're familiar with this case enough to properly evaluate the situation.'

26

'For starters,' Peck said, producing a business card from his shirt pocket, 'I'm not a doctor.'

' "United States Department of Animal Health and Welfare"?' the nurse read. 'Are you serious? Someone actually called the pound? Look, I think there's been a practical joke played on you. And I know just the guy on the morning shift who probably put this whole thing together.'

I beg your pardon, nurse,' Peck countered, 'but I'm here at the request of the hospital administration, and I'll wager he got in touch with me just in time. We're dealing with a potential epidemic here, I hope you realise.'

By now the nurse was hopelessly confused, and she made no effort to stop Peck from entering Murdock's room. As he was opening the door, however, the orderly burst out at him, almost bowling him over in his haste to flee the dogman in the room.

'He's crazy! I mean gone!' the orderly gasped, barely managing to close the door before Murdock could scramble out into the hallway.

'Did you give him the shot?' the nurse asked.

'I tried, but the damn guy bit me!' The orderly quickly displayed the chomp marks on his hand, then went back to massaging the wound with his other fingers. 'And he's foaming at the mouth, too! Forget the needles, the only thing I'd try shooting him with now would be a shotgun. Both barrels.'

'I can't believe it!' The nurse looked at Peck, flabbergasted. 'He's never been this violent before!'

'Just leave him to me,' Peck said with calm authority, grabbing an untended trolley a few yards down the hall from him. 'In the meantime, I'd advise the both of you to go in for a series of blood scans, along with full tetanus and rabies shots if you haven't had either in the past three years. I don't have to tell you the spread rate on something like this once it's allowed to get out of hand.'

'But how can he really have rabies?' the nurse protested, clinging to her last shred of coherence. 'His dog isn't real, and he really isn't a dog. . .'

'You haven't been briefed on this at all, have you?' Peck said, letting a trace of irritation slither into his voice. 'We think he must have contracted it from the escaped animals last night when they were in the area.'

'Escaped animals?' the orderly said.

'Coming in on a Lufthansa flight from Germany. They were supposed to be transported under airtight security to the Wadsworth Research Facility in Pacific Palisades. They never made it.' While the two workers were digesting this news, Peck set his satchel on the trolley and snapped it open, then pulled out a box of animal crackers. 'I know it looks silly, but it calms 'em right down. Now, grab the door and stand back. If I have plenty of room to work, we should all come out of this okay.'

The nurse stood off to one side while the orderly jerked the door open and Peck rolled the trolley into Murdock's room. As soon as Peck was in, the orderly closed the door and backed away from it as if it were radioactive. Neither he nor the nurse said anything for several seconds. They listened dumbly to the commotion taking place on the other side of the door. Peck wasn't saying anything, but they could hear Murdock thrashing about the room as if he were a werewolf and Peck had just wheeled in a full moon.

'Poor bastard,' the orderly finally muttered as he rushed over to the far wall and tugged down a fire extinguisher from its bracket mounting. 'I wish I had that shotgun, but I gotta use something on Murdock before he mauls that other guy to death.'

'Be careful,' the nurse urged.

Before the orderly could carry out his mission of mercy, the door to Murdock's room opened from within and Peck wheeled out the trolley, unscathed from his supposed ordeal. Murdock was crouching on all fours atop the trolley, a muzzle ensnaring his face. Foam continued to fleck his lips as he growled through his bound jaws.

'Oh my God,' the orderly gasped, staring at his bite with newfound horror.

'You,' Peck said, pointing to him, then to the room that

28

had just been abandoned. 'Inside.'

'What?'

'C'mon, c'mon, inside! I'm trying to save your life, damn it!' The resoluteness in Peck's voice cut through the orderly's doubts and he went into Murdock's room. Peck quickly slammed the door on him and shouted, loud enough for him to hear, 'I want you to remain in quarantine until I can check back with you in a couple of days. Hopefully by then we'll have developed the serum you'll need. You're to speak of this to no one but the nurse here. Is that understood?'

Through the door came the muffled response of the orderly. 'What could happen to me?'

'You're better off not knowing.' Peck locked the door and handed the key to the nurse as he whispered to her, 'Contact me immediately at the number on the back of my card if he should develop any strange symptoms.'

'Such as?'

'He might think he has fleas,' Peck adlibbed. 'Or he'll walk around in a tight circle, then lay down on the floor with his tongue hanging out. That's all I can tell you right now. I have to get this patient to our labs immediately.'

Peck fed Murdock another biscuit through the muzzle, then started pushing the trolley down the hall toward the nearest exit. The nurse followed close behind, sputtering, 'But. . . but. . . wait. Mr Murdock is a patient here. I can't release him to someone from the dog pound. . .'

'We happen to be a division of the Federal Government, working in conjunction with the Department of Health Services, which gives us authority over any and all state institutions,' Peck intoned officiously, 'so please be careful when you go coughing up the word 'pound' like that.'

'I. . . I'm sorry.' The nurse didn't know what else to say.

At the doorway leading out to the parking lot, Peck paused long enough to thrust a set of forms on the edge of the trolley closest to the nurse. 'And I need not remind you to speak of this to no one. All hospitals in the city are on the alert in case of a full outbreak. We don't want a wide scale panic on our hands, do we? Please sign this for me. . .'

The nurse scribbled her name on the form and shook her head. 'I hope Mr Murdock's condition can be caught early enough to develop a serum.'

'So do I, nurse,' Peck said. 'So do I. This man could single-handedly save the entire population of Los Angeles.'

Murdock barked at his prospects of glory.

FOUR

'Too bad Amy's not in town,' B.A. said as he drove his coveted van through the city streets towards Mickey's worksite. 'I bet she could rustle up some dirt on this Denham dude so he could end up behind bars after I put him in the hospital.'

Hannibal was riding next to B.A. in the front of the van. Mickey and Randy were in the back, within earshot of B.A.'s remarks. 'Amy?' Randy asked. 'Who's she?'

'A friend,' Hannibal said, blowing smoke from his cigar out of the window. 'She's out of state at the moment, so she can't be of much help to us.'

'I wonder what Face's excuse is,' B.A. grumbled. 'He missed our rendezvous at the studio, man. Gotta be that fool Murdock slowed him down. I think we shoulda just left that nutbar out of this. He's nothin' but trouble!'

'I like to think of him as more of a catalyst,' Hannibal mused. 'I mean, look at the way he gets the adrenalin pumping through your veins, B.A. He's the next best thing to steroids, and he's totally organic.'

'He's totally crazy, man!'

'Who's Murdock?' Mickey asked. 'How many are there in your gang, anyway?'

Hannibal tapped ash out of the window, then swung around in his seat and eyed the Sterns. 'I guess maybe it's time we got into the small print on our working agreement. Item one, we don't like a lot of questions about the

31

way we operate. If you hire us, it's going to be for results, not a feature story in People magazine. Are we clear on that?'

Mickey and Randy looked to one another. Mickey spoke for both of them. 'Look, if you guys can help us out, you can call all the shots you want.'

'Good.' Hannibal smiled broadly, wedging his cigar back in his mouth. 'That's the way I like it.'

'I think we're here,' B.A. said, pointing out the windshield at the worksite. He pulled into the lot, which was still scarred with the remains of the demolished Airstream. Mickey and Randy scrambled out the van and gasped in unison at the sight before them.

The two henchmen who had accompanied Carl Denham the night they'd blown up the trailer were standing in the bed of a Denham Construction pickup with four other associates of similar build and temperament. The henchmen were addressing Mickey's work crew as they finished their lunch break. They each had their names stitched on the pockets of their work uniforms. The taller of the two was named Boyle. His partner was McGreavey, who had just leaned over the edge of the truck to hand a clipboard to Mickey's employees while Boyle did the talking for them.

'You got until tomorrow to think it over, then the offer's no good.'

'What the Sam Hill. . .' Mickey fumed, striding over to his nemesis's pickup. 'What do you think you're doing here?' he demanded of Boyle and the others. 'Get off this lot!'

'I just do what Mr Denham tells me too,' Boyle replied smugly.

'Around here you do what I tell you!' Mickey roared, stabbing a forefinger past Hannibal and B.A. at the street. 'Now get outta here! I ain't gonna tell you again!'

Boyle smirked and glanced at his cohorts. They all shared an undercurrent of hostile mirth, making light of Mickey's threat. With feigned sincerity, Boyle said, 'I was just bein' kind enough to offer up jobs to anyone who wants 'em once Denham Construction takes over this contract. . .'

'He's not taking over this contract!' Mickey bellowed. 'And these men are on my payroll, damn it!'

'What payroll?' Boyle asked. The challenge silenced Mickey, and Boyle turned his attention back to the men working on the site. 'You guys done signing that roster?'

One of the workers handed the clipboard back to McGreavey, then turned his head quickly to avoid meeting Mickey's withering gaze. Boyle and McGreavey jumped down to the ground, but before they moved to get into the pickup cab, they stood together and gloated at Mickey's exasperation. Boyd took the clipboard from his partner and glanced over the names.

'By my count, they've all signed up, Mick buddy,' Boyle chortled. 'What do you expect? They got families. Denham can keep 'em working. He can also keep 'em from ever workin' again. You should feel proud that they're all smart enough to make the right decision.'

As discreetly as possible, Mickey slipped a nitro into his mouth as a precaution against his rising temper. Then, with the last of his patience, he told Boyle, 'All right, you said what you had to. Denham doesn't have this contract yet, which leaves me in charge of this area. Like I warned you before, I think you better move it.'

'When I'm finished, old man,' Boyle shot back. 'I'll leave when I'm good and ready.'

'Hey, I can still whip your butt like it was mashed potatoes, pal,' Mickey said as he started to roll up his shirt sleeves. 'Come on, let's settle this one on one. . .'

'Uncle Mickey!' Randy cried out, pulling him back before he could take a step Boyle's way. 'No!'

B.A. moved in to take Mickey's place, setting himself directly in front of Boyle. He put his hands on his hips and bored his dark eyes into the taller man. 'The man said for you to go. Go!'

'I take my orders from Denham,' Boyle responded coolly. 'Be smart and do the same.'

'Go to hell,' Mickey muttered, shaking his niece's hands

from around his arm.

Boyle pretended not to hear Mickey's curse. He looked B.A. and Hannibal over, then held out the clipboard to them. 'You guys look like you can work steel pretty well. Sign in and you're on the roster.'

Hannibal took the clipboard and glanced over the top sheet as if he truly was interested in signing it. Then he ripped the sheet off and handed it to B.A., who crumpled it into a bite-sized ball and popped it in his mouth.

'Got another offer you'd like us to chew on?' Hannibal asked Boyle.

'Cute, real cute.' Boyle watched B.A. swallow the wadded sheet, then narrowed his eyes as he looked back at Hannibal. 'Look, if you're thinkin' of workin' for Stern here, maybe you oughta first ask the rest of his crew about how dangerous it can be around here. I understand there's a dark cloud raining bad luck on this place night and day.'

Hannibal flicked the butt of his cigar into the dirt between Boyle's feet, then blew a last breath of smoke into the other man's face. 'Maybe we'd like it better if you told us about this bad luck. Why bother with a middle man, eh?'

'It's easy to get hurt around here,' Boyle said.

'That a fact?' Hannibal said. 'Then maybe you and your boys better leave as quickly as possible.'

'Nothin's gonna happen to us.'

'Oh? The bad luck's kinda selective then, is it?'

'That's right. And I see some of it coming right your way if you don't wipe that damn smirk off your face! It bugs me, dig?'

' "It bugs me, dig?" ' Hannibal parroted, widening his smirk. 'Hey, I haven't heard that kinda lingo since Dobie Gillis went off the air. You can do better than that, can't you?'

'How's this?' Boyle's arm pumped like a runaway piston, launching a fist aimed for Hannibal's jaw. Hannibal saw it and easily ducked the blow, then jammed the narrow end of the clipboard into Boyle's midsection, forcing the wind from his lungs. Boyle buckled at the knees, gasping for air. Hannibal shoved him to one side and braced himself for the torrent of bad-tempered manpower piling out of the pickup. Beside him, B.A. and McGreavey fell on one another like the main attraction at big-time wrestling. B.A.'s twenty pounds of gold necklaces rattled ominously around his neck like chains in a Houdini routine.

'Don't play with him any more than you have to B.A.,' Hannibal advised. 'I've got four guys who all want the next dance with me.'

B.A. dispatched McGreavey with a few quick rabbit punches, but that still left four opponents for him and Hannibal to contend with. Mickey was tempted to join in the fray, but Randy clung to him, hissing, 'Don't you dare!'

'Can't let them take my licks for me,' Mickey argued, although he made little effort to break free from his niece's grasp this time. Looking past the fracas, he called out to his workers, 'Hey! Give those two a hand! Let's show Denham we can't be pushed around.'

The workers, however, were less than eager to lay a hand on people they thought they might be forced to seek work with in the near future, and they all remained where they were, watching the melee. Commando experience gave Hannibal and B.A. the element of surprise, but they still had to overcome weighty odds against them.

'Now I know how Custer must have felt,' Hannibal groaned between punches.

'If the Faceman was here we might have a chance!' B.A. said, sidestepping a roundhouse right from one of Denham's men and returning a punch of his own that was right on the mark. As the opponent slumped to the ground, he was replaced by McGreavey and Boyle, who had recovered enough to make more trouble.

'You guys are finished,' Boyle said. 'We gave you a chance to wise up, but you weren't interested.'

'It ain't over till the fat woman sings,' Hannibal countered, 'and she hasn't even shown up yet.'

'You're gonna need more than a fat woman to save your

necks,' McGreavey threatened, snatching up a pipe wrench and swinging it at Hannibal's head. He missed, but Hannibal could feel a breeze across his face as he leaned away from the attack.

'Peck! Murdock!' he called out, 'Where the hell are you?'

FIVE

Peck and Murdock were closing in on their destination, whistling along side streets in Peck's new Corvette, a snappy little number he'd picked up as a necessary embellishment for his scams with the motion picture industry. Murdock was out of the muzzle, but he hadn't completely rid himself of his canine tendencies yet. Sitting next to Peck, he munched on dog biscuits from the box held in his lap, popping them into his mouth with the carefree ease of a movie patron feeding on popcorn during a main feature.

'Face, these are great!' he enthused.

'I'm glad you like them,' Peck said, screeching the sports car around a corner. 'They'll do wonders for tartar build-up in your mouth.'

Murdock nodded vigorously as he chomped down another tidbit. 'Do you think they make these in liver? I could use more liver in my diet.'

'I don't know, Murdock,' Peck groaned. 'After we've taken care of business, we'll hit a few pet shops and see, okay?'

'Yeah, super! I wanted to check out some collars anyway. You think I'd look good in something with studs?'

Peck glanced over at Murdock in disbelief. 'Naw, studs are all wrong for you, Murdock. Too macho. You want something more subtle. A sterling choke-chain maybe.'

'Hmmmmmm.'

While Murdock leaned over to inspect himself in the rear-view mirror and cross his throat with his fingers to see what width of collar would best complement his long neck, Peck raced under a changing traffic signal and promptly began pumping the brakes when he spotted the construction site. Hannibal and B.A. were still holding their own against Denham's thugs, but they were visibly tiring. Mickey, Randy and the others had yet to intervene in the conflict.

'Oh, brother,' Peck sighed as he pulled up behind the black van and killed the engine. 'It's almost predictable by now, isn't it?'

'Well, you know how it is with creatures who travel in packs.' Murdock closed his box of biscuits and set it on the floor. 'You get that ol' excitement goin' and the next thing you know, everybody's barking.'

'Ah . . . yeah.'

'You can read up on it,' Murdock insisted as he got out of the Corvette. 'Harvard did a whole study.'

As Peck and Murdock rushed over to aid their counterparts, Murdock scratched himself a few times and gave a few short yips. Peck warned him, 'Don't bite anyone unless you have to, okay?'

Coming up behind the two bruisers who were pummelling Hannibal with a flurry of fists, Peck and Murdock grabbed them by the shoulders and jerked them backwards in such a way that they were thrown off balance. With the precision of drill instructors, Peck and Murdock slammed the two foes into one another, head first. Their skulls connected with a sound like mating coconuts and they dropped to the ground. The odds were suddenly even. Inspired by the arrival of reinforcements, B.A. and Hannibal found their second winds and relied on a display of martial arts to help Peck and Murdock quickly wear down Boyle, McGreavey, and the two other men. Hannibal dazzled Boyle with a combination of moves that ended with a wicked Karate chop that sent Boyle spinning limply into a large wheelbarrow. B.A. polished off

McGreavey and laid the man's inert form over that of his cohort, then wheeled the barrow over to the pickup, where Murdock and Peck were loading hapless opponents into the back of the truck.

'So glad you guys could make it,' Hannibal said as he brushed himself off.

Peck rubbed his jaw, which bore the reddened imprints of several fists. 'That's the trouble with a car like that,' he said thickly, gesturing at his 'vette. 'You're never late for anything.'

Hannibal draped his arms around Peck and Murdock. 'You did great work, boys.'

Murdock let out a cheerful yelp and began huffing with his tongue out like a grateful pup. Hannibal pulled his arm away and eyed Murdock suspiciously as he asked Peck, 'What's this? He's barking now?'

'I'd say it was just an expression of pure enthusiasm,' Peck said. 'You know how happy he gets whenever he's let loose after being cooped up at the hospital.'

'It's like a kennel there, Colonel.' Murdock put on a long face and reached out with one hand, nudging the bulge in Peck's coat pocket as he began to whine.

'Sorry, Murdock, I don't want to spoil your appetite before feeding time.'

Murdock whined a little louder and Peck broke down, reaching into his coat pocket and withdrawing one of the dog biscuits he'd stuffed there back at the hospital. He held it out to Murdock. 'Okay, here.'

Murdock stared at the lone treat and shook his head with sad indignation. 'Face, I find it rather simplistic and naive of you to assume I can be placated with an ersatz morsel of this kind. A shallow, culinary trinket. Honestly.' Murdock stuck his nose in the air and sniffed contemptuously, then added, 'Now . . . if it was *two* of them. . .'

Peck looked over at Hannibal, who could only shrug his shoulders. Peck reluctantly fetched another biscuit from his pocket and held it out to Murdock. Murdock snatched the treats and gobbled them down voraciously.

B.A. had been watching over Denham's men until

Boyle recovered from his beating enough to take the wheel of the pickup and drive off. He witnessed enough of Murdock's antics to catch the gist of his latest preoccupation, and wasn't about to put up with it.

'No way!' he shouted, striding over to Murdock and pinning the lean man against the side of the van. 'You better think twice about bein' a dog, sucker! Bad enough when I gotta put up with inivisible Billy! I hear you bark again and I'm gonna feed you some bones with a lot of meat on 'em.' B.A. hoisted a massive fist and waved it a few inches from Murdock's face.

'Hey, that's another good one, B.A.,' Peck said admiringly. 'I like that one even more than the one about helping Denham with his bridgework.'

B.A. turned away from Murdock and glared at Peck. Meanwhile, Mickey and Randy walked over to join the A-Team while the rest of Stern's crew wandered off. Hannibal noticed their clients' uneasiness in the face of the Team's idiosyncrasies and assured them, 'You know the old saying, the family that plays together stays together.'

Mickey nodded. His face was flushed with traces of shame. 'Hey, listen, I feel bad for standing by and letting you do my dirty work for me. It's just that I've got a bad pump and –'

Hannibal held a hand up to silence Mickey. 'That's okay. We were just doing our job, and when we work, we like to work alone. You only would have been in the way.'

Randy stroked her uncle's back as she asked Hannibal, 'Does that mean you're taking the job?'

Hannibal took a pack of cheroots from his pocket. Half the cigars had broken in half during the fighting. He found a good one and lit it up, then said, 'We know you can't pay up front, so the way we work in this kind of situation is by taking points. How's ten percent of the contract, providing we make sure you get to keep it?'

'That sounds more than fair to me,' Mickey admitted.

'Then we have a deal.' Hannibal offered a hand and Mickey shook it. Circling around to the passenger's side of the van, he told his fellow A-Teamsters, 'Now let's go let our good friend Mr Denham know we're taking care of business here.'

Murdock slinked away from B.A. and crawled into the back of the van. As Peck followed him, he called out, 'Uh, Hannibal, I'm quite sure his goons are gonna pass that bit of data along.'

'Face!' Hannibal admonished. 'Never. . . never allow someone else to do a chore that you can do so much better.'

Before Peck could climb into the back of his van, B.A. intercepted him. 'Hey, man! If I gotta risk my wheels in the line of duty, so do you.'

'Now, B.A.,' Peck said, laughing uneasily. 'I mean, the 'vette just isn't equipped for this kinda work. It's a finesse car.'

'Get in it and follow us!' B.A. said. 'If we get in trouble and somebody's wheels gotta get smashed, it's your turn!'

Peck could see that arguing was useless. Stuffing his hands in his pockets, he headed back to the Corvette. Murdock bounded out and followed him, saying, 'I'll go with ya, Face!'

Peck eyed Murdock cynically. 'You just want me for my dog biscuits.'

SIX

Mickey Stern's construction firm was definitely a David in contrast to Carl Denham's Goliath operation. Whereas Mickey's meagre financial base forced him to provide his crew with antiquated, second-hand equipment, Denham's men worked with state-of-the-art tools provided by the company's underground connections. Five long blocks away from the site where Mickey was contending with his ongoing problems, Denham Construction and Demolition was throwing up the framework for what would be a ten-storey condominium a mere stone's throw from the beginning of the Wilshire Corridor. Half the crew were still at work, manning machines and scrambling about the beams and girders. A dozen other men, including the handful that had just taken a drubbing from the A-Team, were lingering around a catering truck parked a few dozen yards from the lean, gleaming trailer that served as the project headquarters. Boyle, McGreavey and the others were quiet and sullen as they ate, trying to ignore the light-hearted jibes of their fellow workers. There were a few black eyes and bruises, but no severe injuries, except to the men's sense of pride.

Over in front of the trailer, however, a less-than-subdued confrontation was taking place between Denham and a wiry, lethal-looking man in a seersucker suit who obviously belonged to the stretch limousine parked next to the trailer. Crazy Tommy T handled most of organized crime's ties with the construction business, and he was the only man Denham dealt with that he even remotely feared. Denham knew why they called Tommy Crazy, and he always made a point not to press the man's trigger temper, because when Crazy Tommy T lost his temper, men were known to lose their lives, often for just being in the way when Tommy vented his rage. Right now Tommy looked like someone made out of dynamite and Denham looked like a reluctant fuse. Even Tommy's chauffeur was standing at the far side of the limousine, ready to duck for cover if his boss were to explode.

'I don't want to hear this kinda thing,' Tommy was whispering through the hairs of his drooping moustache. His thick eyebrows hung down similarly over his small, reptilian eyes, which were the colour of dull tin pierced by bullets. His whisper carried more menace than most men's shouts. 'I don't come down here to let you tell me your boys got their beanies handed to them. I come down here so you can tell me that building on Federal isn't coming down anymore until you're in charge of the project. You hear me, Carl?'

Denham's lips did isometrics, pressing tightly against one another until the skin around his mouth turned white. He gave his head a terse nod and muttered, 'Yeah, Tommy.'

Tommy rammed a skeletal, ringed fingertip under the base of Denham's chin, forcing Denham to reel backwards into the siding of his trailer. He kept the finger in place, threatening to poke through the soft flesh beneath Denham's clenched jaw as he leaned forward until the pasta on his breath charged up the other man's nostrils from the force of his shouting, 'You hear me!?'

The whiteness spread to the rest of Denham's face. His eyes darted frantically, staring over Tommy's shoulders to see if any of his men were witnessing his humiliation. Only the chauffeur was within sight, and he was well-practised in the art of looking the other way.

'Yes, Tommy, I hear you,' he said through his teeth. 'Loud and clear.' His voice stank of humility.

'You do, you do, but meanwhile I get to drive down Federal and see the walls of that warehouse coming down under Stern's supervision, right?' Tommy pulled his hand away from Denham's face and spun around, heading back to his limousine. His chauffeur quickly circled around and opened the back door while Denham rubbed the raw spot under his chin, simultaneously relieved that he hadn't been harmed any more and enraged that he'd been ridiculed out in the open. Tommy paused before he climbed into his limo and glared back at Denham. 'Every day I have my driver swing out of our way to take a peek at that site, and you know what I see, Carl? Hmmm? What do I see?'

'You just told me,' Denham replied sullenly. 'I know what you see.'

'Well, you damn well better make sure I start seein' something else,' Tommy shot back. 'I want Stern off that job and you on it. And not next month or next week. I want results now! I want you to stop him. Capish? If you can't handle the job, maybe it's time I took my business elsewhere. Maybe someone else around town might like to have me bankrolling them, don't you think?'

As Tommy climbed into the leather interior of the limo and the chauffeur closed the door on him, Denham took a deep breath and came over. He leaned over and motioned for Tommy to roll down his window. Tommy pressed a button and the smoked glass whirred into the framework of the door, revealing his scowling countenance.

'Look, Tommy,' Denham promised, 'I swear to you, it's all gonna be taken care of there by tomorrow. Stern's comin' up to payday, and I know for a fact that he can't come up with the bread for his men. Nobody can afford that kinda charity, to keep working for nothing. They got families to feed and rents to pay. I guarantee you, as of tomorrow Stern is out of business. Then we step in and take over the contract. This little scuffle with my men was his last hurrah, that's all.'

Tommy fumbled through his suit for an onyx cigarette holder, then fitted a thin cigarillo into it and ignited the tip. Between puffs, he told Denham, 'I *did* see what you did to that poor bastard's trailer, so I know you can get results when you want to.'

'That's right.' Denham risked a smile. 'We're closing in for the kill. We let Stern have his day this morning, just to get him cocky enough so he won't be ready for what we hit him with next. Trust me, Tommy, I got it all covered.

Tommy grinned around his cigarette holder, bearing stained teeth that looked like tarnished pearls. He reached out and gave Denham a friendly pat across the face, 'That's what I like to hear, Carl. That's good, real good. You take over the project and maybe I won't have to set up another kind of contract. . . know what I mean?'

Tommy winked and the limo window rolled up, leaving Denham to stare at his own bleak visage. His smile waned and as the limo pulled away, he reflected on Crazy Tommy's implicit warning. He knew damn well what kind of contract the kingpin had been talking about. It was the kind of contract that ended up with somebody being fed to the fish or dumped into a ditch on a country road.

'Not me,' Denham whispered to himself, trying to shake off the chill of fear that had crept down his spine. 'It ain't gonna happen to me. . .'

SEVEN

The site Denham's men were working at was wedged between two existing high-rises, and it was with a brief display of derring-do that Hannibal Smith was able to throw a line across the expanse between the roof of a standing structure and swing to the beams of the future condo. He was wearing a hardhat and false moustache, and a lunch bucket was clipped to his belt along with a few tools to round out his disguise. Straddling one of the girders, he took a camera out of the lunch box and focused the telescopic lens on the figure harassing Carl Denham from within the lush confines of the limo. He clicked off a few pictures of the confrontation below, then set the camera back in the lunch box and withdrew a walkie-talkie. As the limousine was beginning to pull away from the lot, Hannibal activated the walkie-talkie and said, 'Stick with the guy in the stretch chariot, Face. Apparently he makes Mr Denham nervous.'

Peck was sitting alone in his Corvette, drumming his fingers nervously on the dashboard. When he got Hannibal's message, he stopped drumming and snatched up a pair of binoculars. Crazy Tommy T had rolled down hiw window again as the limo rolled by, and as Peck brought the thin man's features into focus, he brought his walkie-talkie to his lips and said, 'You should see this guy's face when he's hot, Hannibal. It makes *me* nervous, too, and I haven't even got on his bad side yet. What are you gonna do?'

Hannibal saw Denham break away from his trailer and head for the lunch wagon. Most of his men noticed and stopped whatever they were doing to form a line near the back of the vendor's truck. Keeping the walkie-talkie pressed against his face, Hannibal retrieved the camera and zoomed in on Denham, then started taking more pictures as he kept Peck abreast of what was happening. 'I'm checking out Denham's petty cash situation . . . seems he doesn't believe in Social Security, F.I.C.A., or Federal Withholding. Chalk one up for Mickey, he was right on that count. Whew, look at all that green! He's paying guys out of the back of that lunch wagon.'

Peck was already in the flow of traffic, following Tommy T's limo. He kept the walkie-talkie on and talked while he drove. 'That's a crime, Hannibal. I guess you're going to have to do your civic duty, right?'

'Exactly,' Hannibal said with a grin. 'I mean, he's undermining everything this country is founded on, for crying out loud! I can't allow that. I'm just going to have to sweep down and get my hands on that dirty cash so we have some proof he's bent as a twig.'

'And you really think this guy'll back off if you do that?' Peck said dubiously, pressing his toe against the accelerator to keep up with the limo. 'Boy, I'm glad I'm not gonna be around for that. Good luck, Hannibal.'

'Right.' Hannibal paused a moment to readjust his moustache so it wouldn't tickle his nose, then changed frequencies on the walkie-talkie so he could get the next phase of his plan operating. 'Murdock, are you there?'

There was a momentary buzz on the receiving end, as if Hannibal had mistakenly tuned in on a bee farm, then Murdock's voice came through. 'Ready with dogged determination, Colonel. My fur's on end and I'm on the scent.

'That's great,' Hannibal said, 'but I didn't bring a bugle to sound the charge, so you're gonna have to be ready and figure out when to join in, okay?'

'I'm just like an abacus because you can count on me,'

Murdock warbled over the small speaker. 'I'm ready to hound that fox till I tree him.'

Hannibal put away his camera and the walkie-talkie, shaking his head. 'Wonderful. Here I go into the Valley of Death with the Incredible Dogman as my backup.'

Clipping the lunch bucket back to his waist, Hannibal carefully made his way along the narrow beam to a scaffolding, which he climbed onto and worked the pulleys until he had lowered himself to the ground. Appearing as inconspicuous as possible, he latched onto the end of the line and watched the activity taking place at the vending truck. Denham was barely visible inside, stuffing cash into envelopes and handing them to the driver, who in turn slipped the envelopes into a napkin to give to the worker at the head of the line. By the time Hannibal had reached the head of the line, Denham had finished his share of the business and was getting out of the wagon. Hannibal quickly diverted his gaze, not wanting Denham to see him and realize he wasn't one of the crew.

'What'll it be, mac?' the caterer asked Hannibal, immediately on his guard when he didn't recognize the man before him.

'How's it goin'?' Hannibal said easily as he surveyed the selection of doughnuts and wrapped sandwiches on display before him.

'Guess I could complain, but it won't be no good, so I won't.' The caterer was anaemic in appearance, with large, pendulous ears and wire-rimmed bifocals propped on a nose that looked something like a dried turnip. He had a tattooed lady on one arm and a misshapen bird on the other. Overall, the man seemed as if he was enduring the nadir of a life that had seen far better times. He sneered at Hannibal and said, 'You just gawkin' at that food or are you gonna eat some of it?'

'The doughnuts fresh?' Hannibal asked.

The other man grabbed one and thrust it in a napkin. 'Dunk it in your coffee and you won't know the difference.'

Hannibal chuckled good-naturedly as he took the doughnut and inspected the napkin. There was no envelope inside it. He looked back at the caterer. 'I was kinda expecting a little something on the side.'

The caterer wiped powdered sugar off his fingertips and tossed the change Hannibal had given him into his cash register. 'You asked for a sinker . . . that's what you got,' he said. 'I don't give free refills on coffee unless you buy the first cup here.'

'That's not what I was getting at.' Hannibal took a bite from the doughnut, which had the consistency of baked eraser. He chewed it down, then dabbed his lips with the napkin and reached to his side, unsnapping the hinges on his lunch bucket. 'I thought today was payday.'

'I don't pay people for eating my doughnuts. They pay me.'

'Well, I already paid you, but since this is such a fine dining establishment, I guess a tip is in order.' Hannibal reached into his lunch pail and pulled out a .22 calibre Magnum. He aimed it at the turnip between the caterer's eyes. 'My tip is that you stand nice and quiet so I don't have to tinker with your sinuses.'

Everyone else had wandered away from the wagon, so Hannibal stepped up onto the framework, which allowed him to lean far enough inside the truck to reach the small safe Denham had pulled his payroll out of. There were several stacks of bills resting on the top shelf, and Hannibal transferred them to his pocket as he kept one eye on the caterer, who had his hands held out from his sides.

'Now this is what I call dessert,' Hannibal said, backing down to the ground, keeping his eyes on the caterer all the while. 'I just hope it won't rot my teeth.'

'A lot more than your teeth's gonna rot,' the tattooed man told Hannibal. 'You'll be dead before you reach the corner.'

'Think so?'

'I know so.'

Hannibal was about to leave the lunch wagon when he

felt the tip of a gun barrel tap against the base of his kidney. 'Freeze,' a man behind him said.

'I'm froze, pal,' Hannibal said. He offered no resistance as Boyle reached around him, taking the money and the Magnum.

'I know every man on this crew,' Boyle told him. 'You ain't one of 'em. Who are you, Jack?'

'I'm the Wicked Witch of the North,' Hannibal responded coyly. 'And when I drop on you there's gonna be nothin' left but a smudge of grease.'

Hannibal sank his teeth into his doughnut as if he didn't have a care in the world. Boyle pulled back the hammer of his gun as he rammed the barrel further between Hannibal's ribs. 'I recognize you now, scumball. You need more than that rug over your lip to disguise yourself, friend. You and me got some unfinished business to settle. What do you think of that? I'll give you five seconds to try talking your way out of a trip to the great beyond.'

'Five whole seconds? You're so kind.' Hannibal turned slightly, enough to have a view past the front of the lunch wagon. He could see Murdock standing across the street, a portable stereo on his shoulder and roller skates on his feet. The two men made eye contact and Hannibal drew a finger quickly across his throat.

'Five. . .'

As Boyle continued his countdown, Murdock snapped into action. Cranking up the volume on his stereo, he lunged forward on his skates and rolled across the street with the grace of a drunken stork. He picked up his momentum, then leapt over a pair of sawhorses in front of the construction site. As he bore down on a small shed near Denham's trailer, the men standing in front of it grew wild-eyed and tried to wave Murdock away.

'Hey, you damn idiot! Get away from here!' one of them shouted.

But Murdock had the volume up to too high to hear their warning. He was also supposedly too absorbed in singing along to the music to bother reading the sign posted on the shack. The sign read: 'DANGER! HIGH

EXPLOSIVES! NO SHORT WAVE OR HIGH FREQUENCIES!'

When the men rushed forward to tackle Murdock, he suddenly developed a trace of finesse on the roller skates and veered sharply to one side, avoiding capture. He turned the dials on the stereo as far as they would go, then hurled the unit at the forbidden shack. He missed striking the building, but his aim was close enough to accomplish its purpose. Inside the shack, a steady bombardment of triggered charges exploded loudly, shattering the walls from within like the fists of a superhuman punching his way out of a paper bag.

Boyle hadn't counted to zero when he heard the explosions. He spun around to look at the shed. Hannibal was anticipating the distraction, and he slammed a quick karate chop against Boyle's wrist, sending his gun clattering to the ground. He kicked the gun under the lunch wagon, then laid into Boyle with a vicious uppercut that knocked the thug senseless. Regaining possession of his Magnum and the money, Hannibal then turned on the caterer and ordered, 'Get out!'

'Hey, okay!' the tattooed man said, unhinged by the wild look in Hannibal's eyes. 'Just don't shoot, man!'

As the caterer was abandoning his land-bound ship, Carl Denham rose from the dirt he'd thrown himself onto in the wake of the first explosion. Boiling with rage, he pointed a finger at Hannibal and shouted to get McGreavey's attention. 'They're trying to rip us off! Don't let them get away with that truck!'

McGreavey grabbed the closest weapon he could find, a length of chain as thick as a garden hose, and charged in the direction of the lunch wagon, where Hannibal was climbing into the cab and starting up the engine. Murdock spotted him and promtply changed his course to intercept, howling, 'Beware the dogs of war!!'

Murdock managed to grab the other end of the chain as he sped by, and before McGreavey could anchor himself, he found himself tugged off-balance. Stumbling forward, he slammed into an unyielding upright beam and fell like a scarecrow that had come loose from its perch.

A few of Denham's men showered the lunch wagon with hurled tools, but none of them struck a vital enough part of the vehicle to stop Hannibal from making his getaway. He drove through a row of sawhorses, sending them flying in all directions, then sped down the street. Behind him, Denham rushed over to his Plymouth sedan and spun its tyres in his haste to back out of his parking space. Two of his cohorts piled into the car with him before he shifted into first and raced forward.

Throughout all this commotion, B.A. had been watching from behind the wheel of his van, which was parked behind a pair of Porto-Johns. He had a Browning pump-action rifle in his lap, but decided he wouldn't need to use it. Firing up his engine, he set the rifle aside and broke from cover, driving past Murdock as he shouted out his window, 'The back's unlocked, you hot dog! Get in!'

'Much obliged, muchacho,' Murdock called out, pumping his legs to pick up speed. Once the van had rolled all the way past him, he hurled himself forward and grabbed the handle of the rear door. With some difficulty, he pulled himself up onto the bumper, then opened the door and crawled into the back of the van, just as a pair of bullets slammed into the spot he'd just abandoned.

'Damn fools are shooting at my wheels!' B.A. railed, flooring the accelerator. 'Man, I *knew* it was gonna happen! Murdock, take this rifle and make 'em stop!'

'Say please.'

'Do it now, fool!' B.A. shouted.

'That's close enough.' Murdock grabbed the Browning and crawled back to the rear of the van. He saw the man in Denham's car leaning out of his window to fire another shot, and he ducked to avoid it. The bullet smashed through the rear window of the van and lodged in the woodwork of B.A.'s speaker system. Murdock quickly took aim at the centre of Denham's windshield and pumped three successive shots. The glass shattered in a series of thick webs that obscured the entire windshield, blocking Denham's vision. As B.A. zipped around the next corner and started to gain ground on the runaway lunch wagon, Denham drove blindly through the intersection, swerving up onto the kerb before cartwheeling over a bus bench and coming to a rough landing on his side. No one inside was seriously injured, but they were trapped inside the crumpled auto and could do nothing to prevent the A-Team from making good on its escape.

EIGHT

Crazy Tommy T did a lot of business from his limousine, as Peck was quick to find out. After leaving the construction site, the limo had made stops at no less than half a dozen different worksites and building supply lots. In each instance, the sleek vehicle had pulled around to the back of the trailer or office where the supervisor worked, then idled as someone stealthily slipped out to converse with Tommy. Envelopes invariably changed hands, and the ones Tommy got were much thicker than those he gave out, not surprising since wads of currency tend to take up more room than a list of 'suggestions' for Tommy's partners to incorporate into their upcoming work weeks. It took Peck all of his training and experience to keep up with Tommy's rounds without revealing the fact that he was trailing the gangster. The binoculars helped, allowing Peck to keep his distance, particularly during Tommy's carside conferences. Although he was veering back and forth, down various sidestreets and alleys, Tommy maintained a basically northward course, and soon an ethnic flavour began to creep into the surroundings. Smatterings of foreign languages began to garnish billboards and the graffiti on the sides of buildings declared which specific minority gang had claimed a given block as its turf. Finally they were in Chinatown, where oriental motifs dominated both the architectural and cultural make-up of the area. Peck was familiar with the area, in that he and the other members of the A-Team had a ten percent stake in the Golden Pagoda Restaurant, a Chinese food establishment owned by a man whose daughter had been rescued from certain death in Vietnam ten years ago by Hannibal, Peck, B.A., and Murdock. Peck eyed the restaurant fondly as he drove by, making a mental note to check in sometime in the near future to see how the Yeng family was doing.

A block away from the Golden Pagoda, Tommy's limo swung out of traffic and pulled to a stop in front of a cheesy looking establishment called The Mandarin Palace. It had a gaudy exterior choked with neon and artifical plants, along with a marquee that promised nightly entertainment by a crooner that looked like China's answer to Wayne Newton. The chauffeur parked and went around to let Tommy out. Peck looked on with amazement from his parking spot down the street as a tall, leggy blonde emerged from the back of the limousine with Tommy.

'Where did *she* come from?' he muttered to himself. Focusing his binoculars on the woman's generous endowments, he hummed quietly. 'No wonder he doesn't mind spending so much time in that limo.'

From what he'd watched of Tommy's activities, Peck had a hunch who he might be dealing with, but after all this trailing he wanted to make sure. Concocting a quick scheme, he slid out of his Corvette and removed his wallet from his back pocket as he crossed the street. The chauffeur was leaning over a rack of newspaper vending machines, and Peck hurried by him before the driver had a chance to see him. Heading up the entranceway to the Palace, Peck walked past a gauntlet of bronze-cast samurais holding their swords aloft in such a way as to form an archway. Considering who he was following, Peck eyed the figures suspiciously, half expecting one of them to suddenly lower a sword to bar his way and demand some sort of a password before letting him enter the club. As it was, though, he encountered no resistance until he was inside. There weren't many people about at this time of day, but a waitress was at the maitre d's stand, attaching the day's listing of specials to the restaurant's menus. She had oriental features, but her voice was strictly Southern Californian.

'Good afternoon,' she said as she took a step away from the podium and blocked Peck's way.

'Good afternoon,' Peck told her, matching her smile with his own.

'We're not open yet,' she explained. 'At seven –'

'Actually. . .' Peck displayed his wallet. 'A gentleman who just came in here dropped this outside. He's thin, snappy dresser, dark complexion . . . kinda mean looking. Had a woman on his arm.'

'That's the owner,' Leann explained, reaching for the wallet. 'I'm sure he'll be pleased to have this returned to him. If you just give it to me, I'll see that –'

Peck pulled the wallet back. 'I really think I should hand it over personally . . . I mean, in case there's a reward or something, you know what I mean?'

The waitress nodded demurely and pointed into the main room of the restaurant. 'Mister Tillis is over at that far booth.'

As Peck was thanking the waitress for the information the chauffeur entered the restaurant and strode purposefully towards the podium. Peck cringed, trying to appear nonchalant. The driver walked past him, winking at the waitress. To Peck's relief, the woman said nothing about the wallet. Peck turned and followed the chauffeur across the restaurant to a booth where Tommy had settled next to his lady friend, who was squirming up next to him like some dazzling parasite.

'Tillis, Tillis, Tillis.' Peck muttered the name under his breath until it rang a bell in his brain. It wasn't a pleasant revelation. 'Oh, no. Why him?'

Hanging a quick right, Peck ducked into the side hallway leading to the restrooms. There was a pay phone next to a carved dragon, and he put through a quick call to Mickey's construction site. He got an answer on the fifth ring. It was Randy.

'Hello?'

'Hi, Randy? It's Peck. I need to talk to Hannibal. Is he there?'

'Yes!' There was cheer in Randy's voice. 'He's paying my uncle's men for their work with money he got back from Denham. Isn't that wonderful?'

'Marvellous. How about if you let me congratulate him on a job well done?'

'Just a second. . .'

As he waited for Hannibal to get on the line, Peck looked around him, trying to locate the nearest exit in the event of him feeling the need to leave in a hurry. He was having his doubts about coming into the restaurant. He felt a little like Jonah crawling into the belly of the whale to make sure it was really as big a creature as he'd suspected. A bad case of overdedication.

'Face,' Hannibal's voice came over the line. 'We came through on our end. How's it going with you? You still tailing that guy?'

'That guy happens to be Tommy Tillis.'

'Tommy Tillis? Crazy Tommy T?'

'The one and only,' Peck said. 'Hannibal, that guy's Mob City, and I'm in some restaurant he owns just down the block from the Golden Pagoda.'

'Good job.'

'Are you kidding? Hannibal, the place isn't open yet. The only people here besides me are him, a couple of ladies and this chauffeur who looks like a stand-in for Godzilla. I could end up on the menu if I don't watch it!'

'Then watch it, Face. Nothing to it. Now, the quiz question of the day is how's he connected with Denham? And why the pressure to keep Mickey here from getting on with his job.'

'Whatever the reason, I don't think we wanna get in this guy's way,' Peck whispered into the receiver. 'I've heard stories about this Crazy Tommy. He hits a wall head-on and there's nothing left but a pile of bricks.'

'Be careful, then,' Hannibal told him. 'As soon as B.A. finishes paying off the crew I'll take him and Murdock and check out Denham, see how he's taking this last slap in the face we gave him. You stick to Tillis. See what else you can find out.'

'Stick with. . .' Peck shook his head. 'Hey, Hannibal, I didn't plan on making this a career. The guy makes more rounds than the Avon Lady, and if I'm lucky enough to get out of here in one piece, it'd only be a matter of time before he got wise to my 'vette. Face it, that's not the most inconspicuous car to do a tail job in.'

'Maybe that'll work in your favour. He'd never think anyone would be stupid enough to try tailing him in something that flashy.'

'Come off it, Hannibal. You don't believe that.'

'No, but I thought saying it might make you feel better. Look, Face, we'll be out on the road shortly. If you can, how about leaving a message with Sam Yeng over at the Pagoda. I'll stop by or give him a call later.

Peck hung up the phone, not feeling any better than he had before he called. He saw the flickering of an exit light around the corner and started for it. He didn't get far. After two steps, his forward progress was impeded by the sausage-sized fingers that dug into his shoulder and pivoted him around. The chauffeur eyed him with an expression Peck often used on houseflies the moment before he laid into them with a swatter.

'Hi!' Peck said with false cheer. 'I was just passing through. You know, put a quick call into my broker, sell off a few bad stocks before the end of trading.'

'Mr Tillis wants a few words with you.'

'Me?'

'You got it.' The behemoth driver dragged Peck out of the hallway and shoved him in the direction of the booth where the waitress was serving drinks to Tommy and his playmate. The waitress eyed Peck coldly, then moved away, giving the chauffeur room to guide his captive into the booth. Peck plopped down roughly across from Tommy.

'Ah. . . nice place you have here,' Peck said, admiring the dining room. 'Very tasteful. I especially like the plastic koi fish mounted on the walls. Nice touch.'

'Cut the crap.' Tommy stabbed an ashtray with the last of his cigarillo and pried the butt out of the onyx holder. 'I understand you supposedly have my wallet.'

'Your wallet?' Peck made it sound as if he'd just been accused of being from another planet.

'Yeah.' Tommy glanced over at the waitress. 'Isn't that what he said, sugar?'

The waitress nodded, then drifted away to tend to other matters.

'Right, right,' Peck confessed, trying to think fast. 'Yeah, well, see, I made a mistake.'

'A big one,' the driver droned.

'It wasn't your wallet, then?' Peck asked Tommy innocently.

Tommy shook his head and held his hand out across the table. 'I could be wrong, though. Why don't we double check?'

When Peck hesitated, the driver leaned over and grabbed the billfold from his coat pocket and handed it to Tillis. 'Here, boss.'

'Thanks, Jilly.'

Peck looked up at the driver. 'Jilly? Interesting name.'

'You don't like it?' Jilly asked sinisterly.

'Oh, I love it,' Peck said. 'What's it short for?'

'Jim.'

'I see. . .'

Tillis looked the wallet over, making a sour face, as if he found it contemptible that someone wouldn't bother to buy a new billfold the moment his old one had faded as much as Peck's. 'You're right, this isn't mine.'

'Good,' Peck stretched his hand out to retrieve it as he started to stand up. 'Now that we've cleared all this up, I'll just be on my way.'

'You ain't goin' nowhere, friend,' Jilly said, pushing Peck back down into the booth. 'Not till Mr Tillis says.'

'Of course,' Peck laughed uneasily. 'How rude of me. I tell you, at the orphanage they just didn't spend as much time emphasizing etiquette as they should have –'

'Shut up!' Jilly commanded.

'No, Jilly,' Tillis corrected as he leafed through Peck's bulging wallet. 'We want him to sing us a song. Something in the top ten. Something we'll like to hear.'

'The truth is,' Peck said, 'my voice isn't what it should be.'

Tillis pulled out one of Peck's business cards and read, ' "Maury Birnbaum?" Hmmmmm, a talent agent, eh?'

The woman next to Tommy acted as if someone had finally inserted some batteries into her power pack. She batted her eyelashes at Peck and showed off her rows of capped and creamy teeth. Her delicate fingers began to fuss with a pendant dangling from her neck, the better to draw attention to the cleavage displayed above the top seam of her low-cut dress. Peck decided to play along with the moment, conjuring up some prime chutzpah.

'I'm sorry, hey, what can I say? I mean. . . this woman is gorgeous!' he oozed boldly. Staring wistfully at the blonde, he cooed, 'I don't know who's representing you, doll, but you deserve a lot of exposure.'

The woman twittered, 'If I exposed myself any more Tommy'd kill me!'

Tillis pulled a handful of cards out of Peck's wallet and read another one of them. ' "Arturo Wainwright, tractor salesman"?'

Peck smiled uneasily. 'Yeah, well –'

' "Herbert Digby, coffin salesman",' Tillis read on the next card. ' "You just ask it, we've got the casket"?'

'Not exactly my idea of great poetry either,' Peck said.

Tillis dropped the cards and the wallet on the table before him, then busied himself with reloading his holder with another cigarillo. He spoke to Peck without looking at him, his voice like the calm before a bad storm. 'You either have trouble holding down a job, ace, or you're some kind of con artist. I hate conmen! They make me want to puke. Tryin' to con honest folks into turnin' over their life savings. . .'

'Yeah, I know what you mean,' Peck said, 'It's not a glamourous sort of crime. Nothing like, say, protection

60

rackets or rigging construction contracts.' He spilled the words out compulsively, his mouth like a bursting dam. He regretted them even as they were burning Tommy's ears.

Tillis raised his gaze and eyed Peck coldly. 'You better talk to me, and you better tell me something that makes sense, or I'm gonna have Jilly here use your head for an anvil. You know what an anvil is?'

'Okay, okay,' Peck said, as if throwing aside all pretence for the first time. 'I'm sorry, Mr Tillis. I'm J. Pierrepont Finch from the National Insider. Those cards are things I picked up along the way on various assignments. You know how people react to the press. Sometimes you have to come in sideways to get a source to open up to you. I'm sure you've experienced that yourself.'

'What's this you were saying about protection rackets and rigging construction projects?' Tommy asked.

'Oh I just wanted to ask if you'd been victimized by people dealing in that line of work,' Peck explained 'I'm doing this story on crime in the business world, and I thought you might be able to give me the perspective of a respectable owner trying to operate in the midst of so much organized crime.'

Tommy lit his cigarillo and stared through the first arabesque of smoke at Jilly, raising an eyebrow questioningly. Whatever the question was, Jilly answered it by shaking his head. Tommy blew some smoke and looked back at Peck. 'Car keys,' he said.

'Huh?'

Jilly yanked Peck out of the booth and frisked him until he came up with a set of keys.

'Oh, keys,' Peck said. 'There they are. We going for a ride, is that it? You want to go someplace else to talk. Hey, fine with me. Just let me call into the office to –'

'Shut up!' Tommy snapped. He took the key ring from Jilly and started looking through the keys. 'I tell ya, ace, if one of these fits a Corvette parked anywhere outside here, we just might be going for a ride, all right. Because if that

61

car's yours, that means you've been tailing me from that construction site over on Federal.

Before Tillis came to the Corvette key, the waitress returned to the booth, carrying a phone. She plugged it into a jack and set the receiver before the gangster.

'It's for you, Mr Tillis. A Mr Denham.'

Peck winced inwardly as Tillis picked up the phone.

'Yeah, this is Tommy,' Tillis growled into the receiver. 'What is it, Denham. . . what? When? When did this happen!?' In a matter of seconds, Tommy's complexion changed through more colours than that of a chameleon perched on a rainbow.

'I don't think this is good news,' Peck told Jilly as he scanned the room for any possible means of escape. He knew the bulge in Jilly's coat belonged to a piece of hardware that would nail him before he got more than halfway to the nearest exit, though.

'What the hell's goin' on!' Tommy raged after he got the gory details from Denham about the A-Team's raid on his construction site. 'What are we doin' gettin' hit like that? . . . No, no, you stay put, damn it! I'm comin' right over!' Tommy slammed the receiver down and bounded out of the booth. 'Let's go!'

Peck waved his hand in hopeful farewell and told Tommy, 'We can finish up our interview next time. Maybe I'll just stay here a few minutes and chat with the young lady. . .'

'Jilly, bring this shyster along,' Tillis ordered, looking crazier by the moment. 'I think he's in with some clowns that just ripped off a nice slice of my money at Denham's work site. If it turns out I'm right, I want him around to take it out on.'

'I was afraid of that,' Peck muttered as Jilly grabbed him by the collar. 'I don't suppose you'd let me make that one last call before we go.'

Tommy circled in front of Peck and whispered menacingly, 'You're making me angry, pretty boy. You don't want to make me angry. Is that understood? You don't want to see what I do when I get angry.'

'No, I can't say as I do,' Peck admitted.

The woman remained behind as Tommy and Jilly escorted Peck out of the restaurant and into the limousine. Jilly got in behind the wheel and drove off. Peck could see out the smoked window as they passed the Golden Pagoda. Sam Yeng was out sweeping the front entrance, and he looked up at the passing limousine, but because the windows of the vehicle were darkened, he couldn't see Peck, and Peck couldn't do anything to draw the man's attention to his plight.

'So close,' Peck muttered dismally.

NINE

After he had finished talking to Peck, Hannibal put a call through to Carl Denham's corporate headquarters on the north side of town. He got the man's secretary, a formal-sounding woman as devoid of humour as a network comedy executive.

'Denham Construction and Demolition, may I help you?'

'Yeah,' Hannibal drawled, affecting a lazy Midwestern accent. 'This is Norman Mestabol. I'm the new local sales rep for Reddi-Quik Concrete. I'll be making the rounds out your way later on today, and I was just wonderin' if I might be able to meet Mr Denham. . . you know, just stick my head in the door and get acquainted, maybe drop off a brochure. Is he going to be in?'

'Mr Denham plans to be in his office all day, but I'm afraid he's not taking any callers, especially today. If you want to drop off the brochure, though, along with a business card, I'm sure he'll get back to you.'

'Thanks, I might just do that. 'Bye.' Hannibal hung up the phone and stepped out of the booth that was serving as Mickey Stern's communication outpost until he replaced his bombed-out Airstream. Murdock and B.A. were standing nearby with Mickey and Randy.

'Any luck?' B.A. asked.

Hannibal nodded. 'He's going to be licking his wounds up in his office all day. I guess we'll swing by and see if we

64

can't drop a bee or two in his bonnet, eh?'

'I wanta grab some chow first, man,' B.A. said, rubbing his stomach. 'I ain't had more than a few bites all day.'

'I still have plenty of biscuits, B.A.,' Murdock said, rattling his box of dog bones. 'I keep telling you that.'

'I want *people* food, man!'

Mickey offered, 'There's a good greasy spoon around the corner. How about if I buy you guys lunch? Seems like the least I could do after how much you've come through for me already.'

'Thanks,' Hannibal said, 'but I've got a yen for Chinese. I think we'll swing by the Golden Pagoda and see if they've got a stray Peking Duck they can lay on us. You and your niece are welcome to tag along for company, but after lunch we want to be on our own.'

Mickey shook his head and gestured to the worksite behind him. 'I don't want to stray too far. We have a lotta work to catch up on, and I want to be able to do my share. You guys go on ahead and just keep us posted.'

'Thanks again for getting Uncle Mickey his payroll back,' Randy told Hannibal and the others. 'You can't know how much it means.'

Hannibal pulled a small wad of bills from his shirt pocket. 'It means ten percent to us. Come on, Murdock, B.A., this should buy us a nice lunch.'

'Hey, we can eat free at the Golden Pagoda,' B.A. said, snatching the money from Hannibal. 'This is goin' towards fixin' them bullet holes in my van!'

'Easy come, easy go,' Hannibal philosophized as he followed Murdock and B.A. to the van. It was a little before the rush hour so traffic was light and they reached Chinatown in less than half an hour. B.A. parked in front of the Golden Pagoda and the three men went inside the restaurant, which was more humbly adorned than its rival down the block. Because the Yengs concentrated more on offering good food than fancy frills, they did a steady business and had been written up favourably on several occasions in the local papers. A few early customers were seated at several of the booths, and Sam Yeng was in the adjacent banquet room, supervising three bus boys who were putting tables together for a large party scheduled for later in the evening.

'Hey, Sam! Long time no see!' Hannibal called out.

'Hannibal!' Sam was in his early sixties, with a face that swarmed with wrinkles. He beamed at the sight of his silent partners and offered both Murdock and B.A. deferential nods. 'Good to see you all again. You here for next month's payment? That not be ready till next week.'

'No,' Hannibal said, 'Actually, we came to eat up some of the profits. What's good today?'

'Everything good,' Sam boasted. 'I know you like duck, so I get one for you. Sit down, sit down, I bring some beers for you, too!'

As B.A. sat down, he grinned sadistically at Murdock and snickered, 'Maybe you wanna try some hot and spicy dogmeat instead, huh, Murdock?'

Murdock's face went ashen. 'B.A., how can you even *say* that!?'

'Just kiddin', fool.'

'Even in jest, that was a tasteless remark, B.A.'

'What you goin' to do about it, sucker, put me in the doghouse?'

'Okay, knock it off, you two,' Hannibal said before turning his attention back to the proprietor. 'Listen, Sam, you didn't hear from Peck today, did you?'

'Faceman?' Sam asked. 'No, not today. Not for many days.'

'Hmmmmm,' Hannibal thought aloud, 'maybe he had to leave in a hurry. Or he could still be around here.'

As Sam headed off to the kitchen, Murdock asked Hannibal, 'What's up, Colonel?'

'Face was supposed to leave a message here for us. Murdock, why don't you run out and see if you can spot his Corvette somewhere around here. Keep an eye open on any restaurants a block away from here. Tillis owns one of them and we don't want to tip our hand to him, not yet.'

Murdock rose from the table and headed out the door

at the same time Sam returned from the kitchen with three cold beers and frosted mugs.

'So how's things here, Sam?' Hannibal said. 'Everything running smooth?'

For a split second, the creases on Sam's face aligned themselves into an expression of profound worry, but he quickly shoot off the look and replaced it with a smile. 'Nice and smooth.'

'That's good to hear.' Hannibal raised his beer for a toast. 'That's worth drinking to. Go ahead and borrow Murdock's brew for a second. Here's to a grand partnership!'

Sam chinked beers with Hannibal and B.A., then the three men shared a first sip together. The front door opened, but instead of Murdock, a young oriental woman walked into the restaurant, a grim, sorrowful expression on her face. When she spotted the men with Sam, she hurried over to their table.

'Hi, Sun!' Hannibal called out cheerfully.'

Sun Yen nodded tersely at Hannibal, then turned to Sam. 'Father, did you tell them?'

Sam's face grew dark and he said a few angry words to his daughter in his native tongue. She listened with ingrained respect, then excused herself to Hannibal and B.A. and vanished into the kitchen.

'What was that about?' B.A. wondered aloud.

'Nothing,' Sam said.

'Sam. . .' Hannibal reached out and held the man's arm as he tried to walk off. 'Level with us. What's the matter?'

Sam deliberated his words, then said, 'She had a fight with her boyfriend. They will not be married now. That is all.'

'No wonder she's upset.'

'She will be okay.' Sam insisted. 'I go get your food.'

Just then Murdock returned to the dining room, short of breath. He came over to the table and told Hannibal, 'The 'vette's parked out there still.'

'That explains it,' Hannibal said. 'He must still be sniffing around Tommy's restaurant.'

'I also checked around for that limo he was following,' Murdock said. 'It's not anywhere around here.'

Sam overheard Murdock's comment and said, 'What limo you talking about? One owned by Tommy Tillis?'

'Yes!' Hannibal said. 'You know it?'

Sam nodded. 'It drive by here an hour ago.'

Hannibal set down his beer, a troubled look coming over him. 'I don't like it. I got a feeling Tommy got a call from Denham while Face was inside his restaurant. We gotta check this out. Sam, I think we're going to have to eat take-out this time. . .'

TEN

Hannibal's hunch about the whereabouts of Crazy Tommy T proved correct. Arriving at the high-rise building that housed Carl Denham's main offices, B.A. pointed out the gangster's stretch limo, parked in the back corner of an underground garage. Jilly was leaning against the front fender, smoking cigarettes and ogling the waxed beauties in a women's bodybuilding magazine.

'Let's park somewhere else,' Hannibal said. 'I'd hate for you to end up with more peepholes in your van, B.A.'

'Hah!' B.A. snorted as he eased the vehicle out of the garage. 'You love it when my wheels get trashed, man!'

'Now, B.A., that's not true. . .'

'Double hah! What about that time you drove it off the pier down in San Pedro after you let Colonel Decker's gun goons make it look like Swiss cheese?'

'It provided a needed diversion,' Hannibal reminded B.A., 'and it succeeded in saving our necks, as I recall.'

B.A. wasn't appeased. He found an alley parking space and manoeuvred the van into it. 'Yeah, well that's just the tip of the iceberg. I'm tellin' ya, one of these days I'm gonna buy me a tank!'

'Oh, that'd be a real good cover for us, B.A.,' Hannibal sniggered as they got out of the van. 'Nothing more inconspicuous to drive around in than a tank.

Murdock sidled up next to B.A. and confided, 'What I think would be even better, B.A., is for you to invest in a dog catcher's truck. I'm tellin' you, it'd be a great cover, and at the same time we could be rescuing all my canine brothers who might otherwise fall prey to the nets of –'

'Shut up, fool!' B.A. interrupted. 'Man, the only way I'd buy a dog catcher's truck would be if there was a cage in it we could lock you up in!'

Hannibal opened the rear of the van and pulled out a briefcase filled with eavesdropping equipment, then closed the doors. As he led B.A. and Murdock past the parking garage, he said, 'I'm tempted to try to work a scam to distract that gorilla by the limo long enough to plant a bug.'

'It'd take time,' B.A. said. 'Tommy T might come back before we could do it right.'

'Maybe so,' Hannibal reflected. As they passed the garage and came in sight of the office building, something caught Hannibal's eye and he grinned. 'I just came up with a plan. Murdock, why don't you duck inside and find out what floor Denham's office is on. B.A., I'm gonna need sixty bucks of that bankroll you lifted off me.'

'What for?' B.A. said warily.

'Let's say I want to make a little investment.'

B.A. peeled three twenties off the roll and handed them reluctantly to Hannibal, grumbling, 'That's the last I'll ever see of those, I bet.'

'Thanks, B.A.,' Hannibal said. 'Now, I need you to stand guard and make sure Tommy T doesn't make a surprise appearance before we're ready for him. You know what he looks like?'

'I seen his mug in the papers.'

'Good. We'll meet over by those bushes at the base of the building in ten minutes.'

The three men headed off in separate directions. Hannibal waited until his partners were out of sight, then strolled over to where three workmen in coveralls were taking a break next to a scaffolding affixed to runners that ran up the side of the building. He spoke with them briefly, then flashed his three twenties. Each of the men helped himself to one of them, then they crawled out of their coveralls, revealing that they wore shorts under-neath. As the workmen took their money across the street to a hole-in-the-wall tavern, Hannibal put on one of the coveralls and sorted through the equipment in his brief-case while he waited for B.A. and Murdock to show up. They arrived on schedule.

'Tenth floor, Colonel,' Hannibal said. 'Denham's got a whole suite there.'

'No sign of Tommy T,' B.A. related. 'Hey, what's with the coveralls, Hannibal?'

Hannibal handed a pair to both men. 'Put 'em on. We're gonna take the outdoor elevator and do a little eavesdropping!'

B.A. glanced up the side of the building, counting off the floors. 'No way, sucker!' he fumed. 'I aint't goin' up that high! Man, it'd be worse than flyin'!'

Murdock, on the other hand, climbed eagerly into his outfit, bubbling, 'All right! This'll be great! Window washing, province of the truly daring! You'll love it, B.A.!'

B.A. shook his head vigorously. 'Uh uh. My feet stay on the ground, and that's final!'

'We're going up, B.A.,' Hannibal said with calm authority, holding the britches out to his reluctant associate. 'That's an order.'

'Why don't we bug him from inside?' B.A. protested.

'You're stalling, B.A.,' Hannibal persisted. 'Look, Face is probably in danger right now. This is the best way to find out for sure what's going on between Denham and Tillis. We gotta do it.'

'Aw, man. . .'

'Tell you what, B.A.,' Hannibal said, snatching up a portable radio the workmen had left on the scaffolding along with their window-washing equipment. He turned up the volume. 'Just concentrate on the music and don't look down and you'll hardly know where you are.'

'Come off it, Hannibal.'

Hannibal climbed onto the scaffolding, followed by Murdock. B.A. hesitated, then finally pulled on the

71

coveralls and joined the others. He was shaking with fear and promptly clung to the support ropes and faced the glass siding as he closed his eyes.

'Going up,' Murdock chimed, activating the automated pulley system that worked the scaffolding. They rose jerkily for a few feet, then the ride smoothed out and they cleared floor after floor. Hannibal readied his equipment while Murdock whistled along with the radio and stirred up the suds in the bucket of cleaning fluid. He wiped off his squeegie and waved it in the air like a conductor's baton. B.A. remained frozen in place, taking deep breaths to bring his panic under control.

'Hang in there, B.A.,' Hannibal said. 'We're almost there.'

'I'm f-f-f-fine, m-m-man,' B.A. stammered.

When they reached the tenth floor, Murdock stopped the scaffolding and B.A. let out a long breath. Now that they were no longer moving, it was easier for him to bring his fear of flying under control, although he refused to look anywhere except at the draped windows directly before him. While Hannibal went about setting up his eavesdropping equipment, Murdock eased up the volume on the radio and began singing along to the latest mega-hit by Elvis Costello as he lathered the windows with suds. He tapped his foot to the beat of the music and matched the movement with strokes of the squeegie, shaving the suds off the glass, leaving it squeaky-clean.

'Hey, Murdock, quit shakin' the scaffold!' B.A. said.

Murdock stopped tapping his foot, but he rocked at the hips, continuing to make the scaffold wobble as he filled the air with his wretched Elvis impersonation. B.A. summoned the nerve to lean sideways and turn down the radio. Miffed, Murdock stopped what he was doing and put his hands on his hips.

'We are window washers, B.A.,' he scolded. 'Window washers listen to music. It sets up a rhythmn for their work. Honestly, we want to be authentic here, don't we?'

As Murdock reached over to turn the volume back up, B.A. warned him, 'You turn that up, fool, and I'm gonna throw you overboard, got it?'

'I dare you,' Murdock taunted, dancing away from B.A. after raising the volume on the radio.

'That does it!' Disregarding his fear, B.A. lumbered along the scaffolding toward Murdock, who saw the determination in B.A.'s eyes and stopped dancing.

'Hannibal. . .' Murdock wailed hoarsely.

B.A. reached forward, but instead of venting his rage on Murdock, he swatted the radio off the scaffolding with the back of his hand. Murdock leaned over and watched the radio fall, relieved that it wasn't him. B.A. grinned for the first time since he'd boarded the planks. Hannibal pulled his head away from the window where he'd attached the small suction cup of his eavesdropping equipment. He eyed B.A. and Murdock with strained patience.

'I'm trying to do a little work here, guys, know what I mean? Why don't you hold off auditions for the Three Stooges until I'm finished, okay?'

While Murdock sulked and B.A. did a slow burn, Hannibal turned his attention back to his eavesdropping. One the other side of the window, Carl Denham and Crazy Tommy Tillis were embroiled in another of their heated conversations.

'I'm telling you, Tommy, they aren't going to find the body, or the skeleton or whatever it is by now.' Denham sat behind his desk, surrounded by momentoes and other paraphernalia testifying to his power and prestige in the construction industry. That power and prestige, however, paled in comparison to the clout wielded by Tommy Tillis, who paced the carpet in front of Denham's desk, smoking down his cigarillo like a short fuse. Denham shrank back further into his chair and picked up a paperweight in the shape of a miniature steam shovel. He fidgeted with it like Captain Queeg on the witness stand and continued, 'That body's below the sub-foundation, Tommy. Unless they're looking for it, they aren't going to bother going that deep with the demolition.'

'I'm not willing to take that chance,' Tommy said. He

was about to say something more, but he heard a dull thumping outside the window behind Denham's desk. Denham heard it, too, and set down his paperweight as he swivelled around in his seat. 'What the hell's going on out there?' Tommy hissed, circling around the desk and pulling aside the drapes.

The window was obscured by a soapy film, then a squeegie cleared a wide strip of glass, revealing Murdock, his lips rounded as he whistled. A second stroke of the squeegie revealed B.A., who was glaring at Murdock. Tommy didn't recognize them, and Denham only glanced at them briefly.

'Just window washers, Tommy, that's all.'

Tommy grunted and let the drapes fall back into place. His cigarillo was smoked down to the filter, so he crushed it out in the scoop of Denham's steam shovel. 'You know what I think, Denham? I think you keep screwin' up on this job because you don't think you've got much stake in it.'

'You gotta be kiddin', Tommy,' Denham countered, transferring the dead cigarillo from his paperweight to an ashtray. 'Don't you think it's easy enough for anyone to check who put that building up for you? If they find Jules's body, they're gonna know I planted it for you. I'm looking to lose as much as you are, and you know it!'

Tommy dished out a smile that had nothing to do with happiness. 'No, you're looking to lose a lot more. You see, Carl, if that body turns up, you aren't going to be around to prosecute. That's a promise from me to you. You'll be rotting where no one will ever find you.'

Small beads of sweat dotted Denham's brow and upper lip as the threat sank in. The fear constricted his throat, making it impossible for him to speak until he'd reached into his desk for a flask of bourbon. A long drink steadied him a little. He slowly rose from behind the desk, telling Tommy, 'I'll get together a bunch of the guys and go down to see who these guys are that Stern hired out to help him. Once we get them out of the way, the rest will be easy. I'll come through –'

'You've mucked up things enough,' Tommy snapped. 'I'll take care of it myself this time. I already have one of them. He's downstairs in the limo with Jilly. I'm gonna take him out to the country for a little talk, then teach him how to breathe from the bottom of a river, then I'm gonna come back and shut down Stern and anybody he's got trying to get in my way. And I want you comin' along. Maybe you'll learn something.'

Outside the building, Hannibal pulled away the suction cup and turned off the microcassette recorder he'd used to tape the conversation in Denham's office. 'Get us down, right away,' he told Murdock.

'What's up?' B.A. asked.

'I found out why they don't want Mickey to be the one who takes that building down,' Hannibal explained quickly. 'I also found out why Face never got around to leaving a message for us. . .'

ELEVEN

Templeton Peck held his breath until his face began to change an ugly shade of red, then stretched his legs out and kicked as hard as he could against the limousine window. He was bound and gagged in the back seat and he had decided that if he didn't try to do something to alter the course of events, he was going to be personally finding out if there was such a thing as reincarnation. He was content with being Templeton Peck for the time being, and he wanted to put off a change of identity for at least a few more decades.

As he was kicking the window a second time, Jilly pulled the door open and glared in at him over the barrel of his drawn gun.

'Mr Tillis doesn't like it when people put their feet on his furniture,' Jill advised with cool malice. 'Knock if off.'

Peck squirmed on the seat, putting on a convincing show of somebody about to succumb to asphyxiation. A bluish hue was mingling with the crimson in his face, and his eyes were wide with terror and desperation. 'Mmmmmpfffff!' he howled through the gag.

Jill either understood gagesse or was able to read Peck's body language, because he leaned into the back seat and loosened the scrap of cloth that held in place the old sock in Peck's mouth. To make sure Peck didn't try anything, the chauffeur at the same time pressed the tip of his gun against the side of his prisoner's head. 'No shouting,' he whispered. 'Any funny stuff and I give your brain air-conditioning.

Peck nodded that he understood. Jilly took off the gag and Peck sucked in air greedily. Between breaths, he gasped, 'Thanks, Jilly. I hate being such a bother, but I thought your boss might be a little upset if he found out I'd died on him before he had a chance to torture me. I know, I know, you don't have to thank me.'

'Shut up.'

'Hey, look, let me ask your something, Jilly.'

'I said to shut up!'

'Hear me out. There's something in it for you.'

Jilly's eyes narrowed with suspicion. 'Like what?'

'For starters, try pulling up my right trouser leg and checking inside my sock.'

Jilly thought it over, then snorted with contempt, 'Why? So you can try to kick me in the face?'

'No, so you make yourself a quick hundred dollars richer. . . and hopefully realize there's a few more favours I can throw your way.'

'You're sayin' you keep a hundred bucks in your sock?'

Peck nodded. 'I figure if it smells bad enough I'll make sure I only use it for emergencies.'

'Likely story. . .'

'Jilly, I'm tied up hand and foot and you've got what looks like a six-shot Ruger staring me in the face. You think I'm gonna try to pull something against those odds?'

The chauffeur quickly glanced outside the limo to see if Tillis was coming. Assured that he wasn't, Jilly then slowly reached down and raised Peck's trouser leg and checked his sock. Sure enough, there was a hundred dollar bill strapped around Peck's leg, just above the ankle. It hardly smelled, either.

'That's just for starters,' Peck said, noticing greed flicker in Jilly's eyes like matching pieces of fruit on a slot machine. 'Suppose that when Tillis got back here, you and I were sitting side by side here, sharing a drink from this back seat bar because you'd just managed to convince me to throw in with you guys. Think about it, Jilly. I know your type. You've probably been a chauffeur longer than you like, and you've been waiting for a chance to prove yourself so that Tommy'll start cutting you in for a bigger slice of the action. Being hired help isn't good enough for you, am I right?'

Peck couldn't have pegged Jilly any better if he'd had telepathy. The chauffeur tried to put on a poker-face, but his eyes gave him away again, betraying secret dreams that had been brought out of hiding by Peck's accusation. 'Tell me more,' he said as he slipped the hundred into his pocket.

'I'll meet you halfway, Jilly,' Peck said. 'You wanna treat me like a hog-tied steer or a future business partner? Don't take too long thinking about it, because this offer's void if I'm still under wraps when Tommy shows up. Savvy?'

'I got a different idea of halfway,' Tilly said after a moment's deliberation. 'I cut your hands loose, but the feet stay tied and I keep my gun on you until you spell out a few more details.

Peck shrugged. 'You drive a hard bargain, Jilly. Sign of a good businessman.'

Jilly grinned as he took a switchblade from his pocket and popped the blade open long enough to sever the rope holding Peck's hands behind his back. With his arms free, Peck was able to sit up in the seat. Jilly plopped down next to him and closed the door.

'Smart move, Jilly,' Peck said as he rubbed his chafed wrists.

Jilly reminded Peck that he was still under the gun. 'Talk. Who are you with? What's your scam?'

' "What's My Scam?" Sounds like a great idea for a game show, Jilly.' Peck carefully reached forward and pulled aside an oak panel, revealing the limo's well-stocked bar. He withdraw a bottle of expensive sherry and examined it with the affection of a true connoisseur. 'Ah, Mr Tillis has excellent taste, I see.' He opened the bottle and inhaled its pungent vapours. 'Mmmmmmmmmm . . . '58, if I'm not mistaken.'

'Come off it,' Jilly said. 'Even I know sherry doesn't have years.'

'I was talking about the original vintage upon which the sherry was based,' Peck insisted. With his other hand, he reached for his shirt pocket. Jilly stopped him.

'Hold it! What you grabbin' for?'

'A cigar, my friend,' Peck said. 'Sherry without a good cigar is like a job without a future. See for yourself if you like.'

There were two cigars in Peck's shirt pocket, each one wrapped in cellophane. Jilly took them both and inspected them carefully, then handed one to Peck and started unwrapping the other.

'These are prime Havanas, Jilly. You're gonna like 'em.' Peck pulled his cigar out of its wrapper and fitted it between his lips, then withdrew a cigarette lighter from his pocket. He suddenly let loose with a ferocious sneeze, spilling a rampant stream of sherry over Jilly's lap and onto his side of the back seat. Taken by surprise, Jilly swore as he tried to squirm away from the spill. Peck flicked his Bic and tossed it at Jilly. The flame came close enough to the sherry to ignite it, and suddenly the entire back of the car was a mini-inferno.

'And you were afraid it was the cigar that was going to explode,' Peck said, grabbing Jilly's switchblade away from him and leaping out his side of the car. With his feet bound at the ankles, the best he could do was slither to the pavement at first. While Jilly groped for a seltzer bottle to put out the fire around him, Peck cut himself free, then scrambled to his feet. He ran less than a dozen yards before bullets came racing out of the limo and whistling past his head. Changing course, Peck bolted in the direction of the building, only to see Crazy Tommy T and Denham emerging from the elevators. They both went for their guns. Peck hurled the switchblade at them, earning a few seconds with which to change directions again. He bobbed and weaved between parked cars, almost bowling over an old woman at one point. Gunshots thundered throughout the garage as Jilly, Tommy, and Denham started closing in on their prey from separate directions.

'This is no fun,' Peck muttered from his cover behind a concrete pillar. A bullet slammed into the pillar and he just missed being blinded by shrapnel. 'No fun at all.'

As Peck was dodging gunfire on his way to another pillar, the A-Team van suddenly roared into the underground garage. Peck waved his arms and B.A. spotted him. The van veered sharply to one side and screeched to a halt several yards from Peck. The sunroof popped open and Murdock rose like a lethal Jack-in-the-Box, spraying rounds from his submachine gun at the three thugs.

'Fightiiiiiiiiing Doggies!' Murdock screamed above the road of his weapon. 'Barking fury at foes with reckless abandon!'

Inside the van, Hannibal reached over the front seat and threw the side door open. Peck dived in with bullets chasing him like angry bees.

'Welcome aboard, Face!' Hannibal said.

'I'm getting my wheels shot up again on account of you, Face!' B.A. shouted as he shoved the van back into gear and headed back the way he'd come.

Jilly rushed back to the limo and ducked in behind the wheel. Tillis was close behind, and when he flung open the back door, he made a face at the smell and sight of the wasted interior. 'What the hell happened in here?'

'Well. . .' Jilly said.

'Never mind, just get on those bastards' tail and don't lose 'em!'

Denham reached the limo and hopped inside just as Jilly floored the accelerator. The vehicle sprang forward, tossing Denham into Tommy's lap.

'Get the hell offa me!' Tillis roared, shoving Denham aside.

'Sorry,' Denham sputtered.

'You haven't begun to be sorry, you idiot!'

Because B.A. had to make a wide turn to head back towards the street, Jilly had a chance to catch up with the van. As they neared the slope leading up from the garage, the two vehicles were racing alongside one another.

Denham rolled down his window and pumped a few bullets into the side of the van. The van kept going, though, and hurtled through the exit, shattering the wooden swing arm and striking terror into the heart of the middle-aged woman inside the pay booth. As if trying to outdo the A-Team, Jilly raced by the booth on the other side, passing a sign that read: 'NOT AN EXIT. SEVERE TYRE DAMAGE!'

A row of vile-looking spikes rose from the asphalt like the fangs of some subterranean beast with a craving for rubber. The spikes ripped into the tyres with ravenous fury, chewing all four of them down to the rims. The limo pitched wildly to one side, wrapping its front end around a fire hydrant. The water main burst, showering the car with a monsoonish spray. Jilly couldn't get the limo to move any further. The only thing he could get to work were the wipers.

'Downed enemy transport!' Murdock chortled as he pulled himself back in through the sunroof of the fleeing van. 'Us helldogs know our business!'

Hannibal looked at Peck, who was still breathing heavily after his ordeal. 'You okay, Face?'

Peck nodded feebly. Murdock sat down next to him and patted Peck's pocket. 'Animal cracker, big guy?'

'Now?' Peck exclaimed. 'After what I've just been through, you want an animal cracker?'

Murdock cupped his hands into palms and assumed a canine begging position. 'Come oooonnnnnnn!'

Peck sighed and reached into his pocket. He came out with a handful of crumbs and handed them to Murdock. 'Sorry, but it's the best I can do, Murdock.' He asked Hannibal, 'What kept you guys, anyway?'

'Face, I told you to stay close to Tommy T, but don't you think you got a little carried away?'

'It wasn't my idea, believe me,' Peck said. As they reached the corner and B.A. turned onto the freeway, Peck noticed for the first time the coveralls his partners were wearing. 'Hey, I hope those aren't new uniforms we're supposed to wear. They're hardly chic.'

'Go easy on 'em, Face,' Hannibal said. 'If we hadn't slipped into these and scaled ourselves a skyscraper, right now you'd be lying on the ground somewhere waiting for the cops to draw chalklines around you.'

'Well, we're not out of the woods yet,' Peck replied. 'Crazy Tommy Tillis isn't the kinda guy to let somebody slap his face and walk away to tell about it. He'll be after us.'

'I know,' Hannibal conceded. 'When we took on this job, I thought we just had a little jurisdictional squabble between hardhats on our hands. Now it looks like we kicked over a stone and found one of the biggest slugs around.'

'We need a plan, Hannibal,' B.A. said, weaving through traffic. 'And it better be a plan that hasn't got my van as part of it!'

'I think better when I smoke,' Hannibal said, holding a hand out to Peck. 'How about one of those Havanas, Face?'

'I hate to say it, Hannibal,' Peck confessed, 'but I needed the cigars to escape.'

'All of them?'

'There were only two left. Believe me, they went toward a good cause, namely my livelihood.'

'Oh. . . that's too bad.'

'Here, Colonel,' Murdock said, putting the biggest chunk of biscuit into Hannibal's palm. 'Try one of mine.'

Hannibal looked at the dog treat, then shrugged his shoulders and popped it in his mouth. 'The Surgeon General would just love me for this. . .'

TWELVE

Depending on who you talk to, during any given day there are between several dozen and several hundred hired killers roaming the streets of Los Angeles County. Not all of them are on-duty, some of them haven't plied their trade in years, and still others won't know that this is their calling until the day when somebody waves some money in their face and mentions that there's somebody they know who could use a good, serious accident. The majority of these hit men and women do their work for organized crime, and a large percentage of that majority were familiar to Crazy Tommy T, who himself had got his start by paying unexpected visits to people who had had the misfortune to have a contract taken out on their lives. This being the case, it wasn't surprising that within an hour after he'd put out the word that he was looking for some hardcore muscle, Tommy T was holding court with a dozen soulless killers in the back room of The Mandarin Palace. Between this unholy dozen, one hundred and eighty-six victims had been unceremoniously rubbed out for various infractions ranging from unpaid gambling debts to doublecross business dealings to looking at some kingpin's daughter the wrong way. They were just what Tommy T was looking for.

'Every one of you guys has worked for me before, and you've done your jobs well,' Tommy said above the muffled din of the singer who was performing on the other side of the wall. He made a point not to include Jilly or Denham in his complimentary gaze. Those two men stood off in the shadows, grateful to be alive and hopeful for a final chance to prove their worth.

One of the killers, a gaunt man dressed in black and known only as Cormorant, spoke above the murmurs of self-congratulation coming from the men around him. 'Hey, Tommy, if you need all of us, you must have a big target, eh? Who we goin' up against, the damn Pentagon?'

There was a chorus of sickly laughter, and Tommy waited for it to subside before continuing, 'I've got four bozos who've been making my life miserable.'

'Only four?' Cormorant said. 'Hey, you're goin' after sparrows with the elephant gun, man!'

Tommy ignored the remark and went on, 'Their leader's about my age, silver hair, always grinning. Another guy's in his thirties, looks like a Romeo and carries around a deck of bogus business cards. Then there's this wild-lookin' black dude with a Mohawk who drives a black van and –'

'The A-Team,' Cormorant interrupted.

'What's that?' Tommy asked.

'You're talkin' about the A-Team,' Cormorant repeated. Around him, the carefree buzzing of the others ceased, and the expressions on the men's faces changed from amused curiosity to concern. Like Cormorant, they were familiar with the A-Team.

'Who's this A-Team?' Tommy demanded.

Cormorant explained, 'They were commandos together in 'Nam. They got thrown in the brig for some damn reason ten years ago, but they busted out and ended up out here. They're tough stuff. I'm always catching wind of them busting up guerilla armies in Mexico or shutting down biker gangs up north. . . they're the ones who put Tom Angel's heroin business on ice a few weeks back.'

'*That's* who we're dealing with?' Tillis said, recalling the accounts about Angel's run-in with the A-Team. 'Hell, no wonder they've been such a royal pain.'

'They know what they're doing,' Cormorant said.

'They're outside the law, same as us, and they know how to play just as dirty.'

'Well then, it's a good thing I brought you guys in, isn't it?' Tommy paused to light another cigarillo, then resumed, 'This A-Team just paid me a visit a couple of hours back. . . ruined my best car. Before that, they've been giving problems to one of my construction concerns. I got a feeling that right now they're probably over at a worksite on Federal, feelin' damn cocky for the way they've been ruffling my feathers. I want to go over there and pay them a visit, give them a little something to remember Tommy Tillis by. Any of you want to come along and lend a hand, it'll be worth double your usual fee. . . provided things turn out the way I want them to. So, what do you say? Who's coming with me?'

There was a moment's hesitation among the killers as they traded whispers. Then Cormorant took a step forward and said, 'Count me in.'

'Me too,' Black Jack Masters piped in.

'And me,' cried Izzy Bedrow.

One by one, all of the paid assassins joined the ranks of those volunteering for Tillis' proposed showdown. Jilly and Denham emerged from the shadows to make their own commitment, provided Tommy would have them.

'We'll take three cars,' Tommy said. 'I'll drive one. Jilly and Denham, you take the others, since you know where we're going.'

'Sure thing,' Jilly muttered.

'Right away,' Denham said.

'All right, let's go,' Tommy said. 'I want the A-Team dead!'

THIRTEEN

Their spirits buoyed by the arrival of their weekly pay and the renewed possibility that they wouldn't have to consider working for the likes of Carl Denham, Mickey Stern's crew was dismantling the warehouse with zesty fervour, anxious to make up for lost time. The crane operator was working on certain areas of the building with the wrecking ball, while other crew members applied more finesse in the removal of salvageable materials. For the *coup de grâce,* a pair of demolition experts surveyed the layout of the warehouse to determine the most advantageous spots to set off dynamite charges. Several radios blared loudly, and the men sang along as they worked, enjoying themselves more than they had in weeks.

Mickey had his sleeves rolled up and seemed to be in ten places at once, providing moral support for the men and pitching in with the actual labour as much as his frail heart would allow. A constant grin creased his face. At one point he was interrupted by a tall, dark-haired man in a three-piece suit, who had emerged from a shiny El Dorado that had just pulled into the lot.

'Excuse me, but are you Mickey Stern?' the business man asked, raising his voice above the drone of the nearest radio.

Stern nodded and walked away from the worksite, gesturing for the other man to follow him. 'I'd shake hands, but I'm afraid I'm a little on the dirty side. Been a long day. What can I do for you?'

'My name is Leo Densit,' the businessman introduced himself, snapping open the briefcase he carried with him. 'I'm with Plant and Cartwright.'

'Oh, right, the insurance folks.' Mickey's smile began to fade.

'I'm the senior claims representative,' Densit explained as he withdrew a manilla file filled with forms and documents. 'It seems that your firm has had a streak of bad luck lately.'

'I wouldn't call it that,' Mickey said.

'Yes, yes forgive me. You refer on several occasions to sabotage and vandalism here.'

'I like to call a spade a spade.' Mickey's fingers went to his beard. 'I suppose you're here to tell me you're not gonna pay up, is that it?'

'On the contrary.' Densit took a cheque from the folder and held it out to Mickey. 'I believe this was the amount you claimed in your loss statement.'

Mickey stared at the cheque. His eyes went wide and he had to grab for his heart pills to keep his excitement from getting the better of him. 'I can't believe it! This is wonderful!'

'Our investigators concluded that there has been deliberate foul play perpetrated against your operations,' Densit explained. 'We're working in conjunction with the police to pinpoint the culprits and press charges. This vendetta being waged against you has to stop.'

'Amen to that!' Mickey said. 'I trust you guys aren't beating around the bush by going after anybody but Carl Denham, because he's the one behind all my troubles.'

'He's one of the men we're investigating,' Densit conceded. He closed his briefcase. 'Now, if you'll excuse me, I'm just on my way to the district attorney's office to see if I can't get some help out of him, too.'

Mickey quickly wiped his hands off on his trousers and forced his large, calloused palm into Densit's free hand. 'I can't thank you enough, Mr Densit. This means the world to me.'

Densit smiled briefly, then retrieved his hand and wiped it off with a handkerchief. 'Good luck to you, Mr Stern.'

Randy was watching the meeting from a nearby shed, where she was taking inventory of work supplies. As Densit returned to his car, she came over to Mickey.

'Who was that?' she asked.

'Santa Claus,' Mickey mused, holding the cheque out for her to see.

'Oh, my God!' Randy gasped.

Mickey gave his niece a jubilant hug and kissed her lightly on the cheek. 'We beat those guys, honey. We stood up to 'em and won.'

'We had a little help, remember,' Randy said.

'Oh, don't I know it.' Mickey waved the cheque in the air. 'I'm givin' em ten percent of this, too. They deserve it.

Randy looked past her uncle and laughed lightly, 'It looks like they must have heard you. . .'

The A-Team van was racing down the street toward the worksite. B.A. pulled into the lot and braked the van a few yards away from Mickey and Randy. All four members of the team leapt out of the vehicle, looking anything but ecstatic.

'Oh oh,' Mickey muttered. 'Something tells me we might have started getting our hopes up too soon. . .'

Hannibal was the first to reach them. 'Blow the whistle, Mick.' he said urgently. 'Let's get these guys out of here.'

'What? We're just trying to catch up, for cryin' out loud!' Mickey protested. 'What happened? What's going on?'

'You thought Denham was a problem?' Peck said. 'Forget it. He's chump change compared to the monster we just kicked over.'

Randy asked, 'What do you mean? Denham's working for someone else?'

'Bingo,' Peck said. 'Either of you ever hear of a guy by the name of Crazy Tommy Tillis?'

'The mobster?' Randy said. 'Why, he used to *own* this warehouse at one time.'

Hannibal signalled for B.A. to go over and blow the work whistle, then he explained to Mickey and Randy, 'Tommy also made this the unauthorized mausoleum for an ex-partner who mysteriously disappeared the same year this place went up.'

'Jules Hand,' Mickey murmured. 'Yeah, I remember reading about that. . . you're saying Tommy killed him?'

'He's smoother than that,' Hannibal said. 'He probably hired someone to do it for him. My guess is Denham's the one who poured the foundation here, with Mr Hand's bones underneath.

'And that's why they've been trying to bushwhack us all the way down the line,' Randy surmised. 'Tommy wanted only Denham to bring this building down. . . that way they'd have a chance to get rid of the body before anyone else had a chance to stumble on it.'

'Oh Lord,' Mickey whispered. 'You mean we've been digging up a grave all this time?'

'That's one way of putting it,' Hannibal said. 'Now we want to make sure it isn't a grave meant for you or any of your men.'

The shrill sound of the work whistle cut through the air, drawing confused stares from Mickey's crew.

'Mickey, I think you better go explain what's happening as quickly as possible, then get everybody out of here,' Peck said. 'I got a feeling there's going to be trouble coming this way, and we'll need some elbow room to deal with it.'

As Mickey headed off to pass the news to his men, Randy stayed behind. 'Tommy Tillis is one of the biggest mobsters in the city,' she warned the A-Team. 'There's only four of you. He can probably pull together an army.'

'Yeah.' Hannibal smiled slyly. 'The poor bums haven't got a chance. Peck, Murdock, let's go see what kind of battle plan we can cook up!'

B.A. was already looking over the heavy equipment. He stopped in front of a large forklift and stroked his chin as he considered its potential as a weapon. Hannibal came up alongside him and asked, 'What do you think?'

'It'll do,' B.A. said. 'I wanna take a torch to it first, though. Needs a few changes for what I got in mind.'

'Fine, but don't get carried away. We're working on short notice here. There's no time for optional equipment.'

B.A. nodded and headed off to the supply shed for a torch. Murdock was already there, stacking boxes of dynamite and blasting caps in his arms. B.A. noticed what Murdock was doing and moved away from the shed. 'Be careful, Murdock! Those ain't bones to bury in the back yard!'

'I know, B.A., I know,' Murdock said, clenching his teeth as he lifted his load and carried it out of the shed. 'Murdock's Howling Helldogs are experts at demolition!'

Hannibal climbed up into the cab of the mechanical crane. Once he'd familiarized himself with the controls, he started up the engine and swung the crane's large neck around, getting used to the feel of the large wrecking ball suspended from a steel cable in front of it.

'Just like trout fishing,' he murmured to himself.

Peck got in the van and drove inside the shell of the warehouse, then opened the rear doors and started hauling out the A-Team's trove of weapons.

'Remember the Alamo!' he cried out, trying to spur on the others.

'We lost at the Alamo,' Hannibal called out from the cab. 'Try something else.'

'Remember our ten percent fee!' Peck shouted.

'That's more like it.' Hannibal said.

FOURTEEN

It was getting dark. The sky looked like a spreading bruise. The construction site at the corner of Federal and Denomville was quiet. A pair of barricades had been set up to cordon off the area, diverting rush hour traffic to adjacent streets. Three vehicles, however, ignored the roadblock. The pickup truck heading the small caravan rammed through the flimsy barricades and was followed by an oversized sedan and Tommy T's hastily-repaired limousine, which still bore a crumpled front fender and grillwork that looked like a bad set of teeth. When they reached the worksite, the vehicles rolled to a stop and fifteen men burst out into the open and slammed the car doors behind them with the force of shotgun blasts. All the men were armed, and they peered at the looming structure before them, ready to shoot at the first thing that moved. Nothing was moving, though.

Tommy T walked ahead of the others, followed close behind by Denham. 'Some kinda reception we're getting, huh, Carl?'

'Yeah, I don't get it.' Denham glanced at the building's foundation, which hadn't yet been disturbed. 'At least they haven't unearthed the body yet.'

Tommy puffed on his cigarillo, scanning the surroundings one more time. 'Stern musta been warned we were comin' or he'd still be here with the rest of his crew.'

'We shoulda figured they'd run rather than meet us

head on.' Denham eyed the bulldozer near the tool shed and was struck with a sudden inspiration. 'Hey, Tommy, as long as we have the place to ourselves, why don't we get the men to dig under the foundation and haul out what's left of Jules? It wouldn't take more than a couple of hours with that 'dozer and a few jackhammers.'

While Tillis was deliberating the proposition, the door to the tool shed creaked open a few inches. Both Tommy and Denham heard the sound at the same time.

'Then again,' Tommy said, raising his Ar-7 semi-automatic and pointing it at the shed, 'maybe Stern's playing hide-and-seek with us.'

'Hey Stern!' Denham shouted in the direction of the shed. 'Stern, you in there?'

Jilly and Cormorant advanced toward the shed from separate directions, but Tommy waved for them to stop, calling out, 'Let me flush him out.'

There were eight shots in Tommy's rifle, and he emptied all of them into the shed at waist level, ripping fist-sized holes in the wood slats and rocking the door on its hinges until it opened all the way. There was no one inside, however. The bullets had shattered a few tool boxes and demolished the time clock but inflicted no casualties. As Cormorant moved in closer to investigate, a cat suddenly lunged out of the shed and scurried beneath the bulldozer for protection. Cormorant checked inside the shed, then glanced back at Tommy and shook his head.

'No luck here. Must have been that stupid cat.'

'Damn,' Tommy muttered. 'Where the hell are they? Where's this hotshot A-Team anyway?'

A spray of gunfire suddenly pummelled the dirt around Tommy's feet. The mob chieftan sprang back and jerked Denham in front of him to provide a human shield as he stared wildly in the direction the shots had come from.

'Over here, Tommy,' Hannibal called out from the roof of the crane's cab. He rammed another ammo clip into his machine gun. 'What brings you and your buddies here at this late hour? Come to pay your respects to your old business partner?'

Hannibal flattened himself against the roof as a dozen of Tommy's hired guns fired at him. Atop the crane, he was positioned at an angle that kept him out of the path of fire, although several bullets would have plowed into him if the roof of the cab hadn't been so thick.

'You don't know who you're messin' with!' Tommy cried out once the din of gunfire had subsided.

Hannibal didn't show himself, but he raised his voice loud enough to be heard. 'You're the neighbourhood cockroach, and I love to kick bugs like you over and watch you squirm on your back.'

'Talk is cheap,' Tommy said, pushing Denham away from him and reloading his rifle.

'Oh, so you want to bat around clichés, eh?' Hannibal said. 'Try this one on for size. 'Sticks and stones can break your bones', and we're toting heavier artillery than either one of those. Now, we can do this the hard way or the easy way. Inside of one minute my three friends and I are gonna unleash on you like your worst nightmare. You're gonna think the earth opened up under your feet and swallowed you whole.'

Tommy grinned at his men and chortled, 'Guy's real poetic, isn't he?' Then he called out to Hannibal, 'Okay, now what's the easy way?'

'That *is* the easy way,' Hannibal informed him.

'Funny man,' Tommy retorted. 'Hey, I've got one for you. You ever heard of a drink called the Idle Braggart? You take four dead guys, four bags of cement, and mix in the bottom of the nearest river. I think you're gonna like it.'

'Like somebody famous once told me,' Hannibal taunted, 'talk is cheap.'

Tommy's face flushed with rage as he turned to his men and ordered, 'Fan out and get that bastard! I'll triple the fee to anybody who can bring him to me alive!'

As the band of assassins was about to set off in separate directions, a motor coughed into life behind the large sign depicting an architectural rendering of the building that was slated to take the place of the warehouse. Moments later, the sign splintered into pieces as B.A. drove the renovated forklift out into the open. He'd surrounded himself with armour plating, leaving a large enough peephole to see through and a second slot he could poke his machine gun through. At the same time he was bearing down on the largest concentration of killers and firing at them, Peck emerged from his hiding place on the lift's rooftop and added his own bursts to the fusillade. Half of the assassins retreated to the vehicles they'd arrived in and crouched behind them for cover as they returned gunfire; the others dodged behind whatever was closest to them, be it parts of the broken sign or one of the Porto-Johns.

From his perspective atop the framework of the warehouse, Murdock had a good view of the enemy, and he began lobbing dynamite charges like somebody trying to knock down milk bottles at the county fair. There was no carney around to give him a kewpie doll, but if there had been Murdock would have won enough dolls to start a family. His steady bombardment kept the killers from advancing or retreating. They were forced to stay in the vicinity of the parked cars, where they still had to contend with the relentless gunfire coming from B.A. and Peck.

No longer a primary target, Hannibal was able to show himself and empty a round of ammunition at Tommy before he climbed inside the crane's cab and situated himself at the controls. There was no dashboard radio inside the crane, but Hannibal was obviously buzzing to some prime jazz. He found a pack of cigars on the floor and helped himself to one of them. Once he had it lit up, he blew a contended puff of smoke and told himself, 'I just love it when a plan comes together.'

As he put his hand on the operating levers, Hannibal glanced out through the bullet-riddled windshield and saw B.A. closing in on a handful of men who were piling into the limousine in the hope of escape. Before anyone could start up the engine, though, the forklift broadsided the limo. The thick, twin blades of the lift pierced the doors on the passenger side, just missing Cormorant and Jilly.

'Going up!' Peck called out as B.A. worked the controls of the forklift and raised the limousine off the ground. He scarred the roof of the car with another round of bullets, then shouted to those inside, 'Let's see the hardware, boys!'

There were five men inside the limo, and enough of them weren't interested in being shot at any more to convince the others to join them in tossing their guns out the window. Peck counted prisoners and held out five fingers for Hannibal and Murdock to see.

Four other hit men had been wounded by either bullets or shrapnel, and they struggled out into the open, their hands above their heads.

'Nine down, six to go,' Murdock said, grabbing for the last stick of dynamite he'd carried up to the top of the warehouse. Tugging the brim of his baseball cap down low over his brow, he bent over at the waist like a relief pitcher checking signals from some unseen catcher. He saw four men getting into the pickup truck and promptly wound up, whispering to himself, 'Bottom of the ninth, bases loaded, two outs, full count on the batter. . . here's the wind-up, and the pitch. . .'

As the pickup was backing up, the dynamite landed three feet away from its right front tyre. The resulting explosion was powerful enough to upend the truck, flipping it over like a flapjack on the morning griddle. The men inside were too shookup and tangled to be going anywhere.

'Caught the low, inside corner!' Murdock cheered, 'Murdock's Howling Helldogs clinch the pennant!'

In truth, however, the game wasn't quite over. Crazy Tommy T and Carl Denham had managed to avoid injury and the various snares set by the A-Team. Crawling on their bellies through the dirt, they approached the oversized sedan, which had been left relatively unmolested during the pandemonium, although it was wedged between the upside-down pickup and a telephone.

'We gotta get outta here!' Denham hissed as he and Tommy slipped into the sedan.

'Shut up!' Tommy snarled, starting the engine. 'This whole mess is on account of your bungling, damn it!'

Hannibal saw the sedan begin to inch back and forth as Tommy tried to wriggle free for a last chance of escape. Grinning around his cigar, he started working the levers of the crane. With smooth ease, the long trussed neck of the crane swung to one side, dragging along with it the suspended wrecking ball. Hannibal judged the sway of the ball and when it lined up on course with his intended target, he quickly jerked another switch.

Wrestling with the steering wheel, Tommy was finally able to ease the sedan around the pickup. Just as he was pressing his foot against the accelerator, though, the wrecking ball slammed down hard on the front hood, crushing both the hood and enough of the engine to make it sputter to a halt. The front tyres also popped from the force of the ball's impact, further immobilizing the vehicle. Denham and Tillis threw open their doors and rushed out of the car, only to run into the sights of Peck's rifle. Peck squeezed off a full clip in front of the two men, and they threw their hands up in surrender.

'Next time we'll spot you some points!' Hannibal called out from the crane.

FIFTEEN

For the next twelve hours, the headline story on every news broadcast was the mysterious apprehension of Crazy Tommy Tillis and his band of desperados at the construction site near the corner of Federal and Denomville. According to most reports, police officers answering an anonymous phone tip had arrived at the scene and found fifteen of the city's most wanted criminals bound together in a human circle around the half-demolished frame of a long limousine. Because none of the prisoners were willing to talk, the authorities were forced to speculate as to the nature of the initial apprehension. The widespread destruction at the site gave rise to the theory that warring mob factions had staged a confrontation for reasons unknown, and that the losers had been gift-wrapped as a present to the city's crimefighting division. The media had flocked to the worksite, cameras flashing and microphones running, and it wasn't until shortly after noon of the following day that the last of the reporters and photographers had departed, allowing a semblance of normality to return to Mickey Stern's project. On the advice of the district attorney, neither Mickey or Randy had divulged any information to the press regarding the allegations against Carl Denham and Tommy T. The two of them, in fact, had made a point of ignoring the media altogether and concentrating on their work.

At twelve-thirty, an unmistakable black van rolled onto

the lot, followed by a late-model Corvette. The A-Team discreetly emerged from the vehicles and walked over to the catering truck parked next to the bullet-pocked tool shed. They all bought coffee, then moved over to Mickey's station wagon and waited for its owner to join them. Mickey gave a few instructions to his foreman, then whistled to get Randy's attention. She looked up from the insurance form she was filling out on a clipboard and noticed the A-Team for the first time since they had arrived. Both she and her uncle were all smiles as they strode over to meet with the men who had made it all possible.

'Well, one of these days we're going to get back on schedule,' Mickey said. 'End of the week at the latest. I can't tell you guys how good it feels.'

'Look, Mickey,' Hannibal said, 'We're sorry about rearranging some of the furniture around here last night. With that gang Tillis threw up against us, we didn't have much choice but to make a mess. You can take it out of our cut.'

'Don't be ridiculous,' Randy scoffed. 'All the damage is covered by our insurance. I talked to Mr Densit this morning and he said that any compensation is a small price to pay for getting Tillis, Denham, and all those other thugs out of circulation.'

Peck told Mickey and Randy, 'I suppose you've heard that Tommy T's lawyer is trying to get the whole gang released without charges being pressed due to lack of evidence. But don't worry. . . once they get today's mail down at the police station and get a chance to listen to a certain tape Hannibal made at Denham's office yesterday, there's going to be some charges that stick. Those swine are going to do some hard time, make no mistake.'

'I'm not worried about it,' Mickey said pleasantly. 'I figure by the end of the day we're going to be cracking through the sub-foundation and 'stumbling' upon the remains of Jules Hand. I think that should do the trick with them.'

Murdock took a step forward and claimed, 'Of course,

if you were to use a qualified dog, I'm sure you would be able to pinpoint the exact location of the body much quicker.' He paused to buff his fingernails on the front of his jacket, pretending to be nonchalant. 'Now, I happen to represent numerous highly available canines, and I'd be happy to arrange their services. . . for a slight fee, of course. Let's say. . . oh, how about a dozen cartons of animal crackers and biscuit assortments.'

'Hey, you got a biscuit for a brain, Murdock!' B.A. growled. 'Get off that dog kick, wouldya? I don't even *like* dogs.'

Murdock stared at B.A. with puppy eyes and whimpered, 'Awwwwwww, B.A. . . .'

'Lassie, go home!'

Mickey reached into his pocket and withdrew an envelope. Inside it was a stack of twenty dollar bills as thick as most wallets. 'Here's the first installment on what we owe you. I hope you don't mind being paid on time like this, but I've got to keep my overheads down as much as possible.'

'This will do nicely for now,' Hannibal said, quickly counting the money. 'It's always been our policy in cases like this to take payment only after you've cleared enough profit to afford it.'

'And who says philanthropy is dead,' Peck snickered. 'I just love being part of a non-profit organization, don't you, B.A.?'

B.A. only glowered back at Face.

'The next payment should be coming to us some time toward the end of next week,' Randy told the A-Team. 'You plan to be in town that long, don't you?'

'To be perfectly honest with you,' Hannibal said, 'we don't know what our plans are for tomorrow, much less next week. If we're not around, just put our share in the bank and let it grow some interest. I'm sure we'll show up sooner or later. Right now, though, I think we're going to go check on another one of our investments.'

'We own ten percent of the take at a Chinese restaurant across town,' Peck told Mickey and Randy. 'You know, diversify the ol' portfolio.'

'Well, we both want to thank you again,' Mickey said, 'from the bottom of our hearts. Without your help we'd be out of business.'

'It was our pleasure,' Hannibal said. 'You know what they say about us ex-Boy Scouts. We can't go through a whole day without doing a good deed here and there. You helped fill our quota.'

'I'm gettin' hungry!' B.A. interrupted. 'Let's quit yappin' and get goin'!'

The A-Team exchanged one more round of farewells with Randy and Mickey, then headed back to where they had parked. B.A. and Hannibal went off in the van while Murdock joined Peck in the Corvette. Before they could pull away, however, Randy shouted to get their attention, then ran over, waving a hat in the air.

'I forgot to show you guys this. We found it while we were cleaning up this morning. Does it belong to any of you?'

It was an old dusty fedora that had gone out of fashion a good thirty years before. Peck glanced at it and shook his head, but Murdock stared at the hat as if it were the Holy Grail he'd been searching for all his life. He took it from Randy and perched it on his head in place of his baseball cap, then tilted it at a rakish angle. The fedora fitted him perfectly.

'Ah, destiny!' he gasped triumphantly.

'Oh, no, what now?' Peck groaned. He waved to Randy and pulled out into the flow of traffic. Riding next to him, Murdock kept leaning to one side and gazing at his reflection in the rear-view mirror, slowing undergoing a strange transformation. He turned up the collar of his aviator's jacket and tilted the brim of his new hat at even more of an angle. A facial tick began to pop his cheek out at intermittent intervals.

'It was a dog's life on the mean streets of town,' Murdock drawled out the side of his mouth. 'I was ready for a change.'

Peck rolled his eyes and shook his head with resignation. 'Goodbye Rin Tin Tin, hello Humphrey Bogart.'

'You said something, sweetheart?'
'Play it again, Murdock. . .'

SIXTEEN

Sam Yeng had been holding back a few unpleasant realities from the A-Team when they had stopped by his restaurant earlier in the week. Contrary to what he'd told them, the sombre, downbeat spirits at the Golden Pagoda were due to more than the romantic tribulations of his daughter. A lot more. Like many other business owners in Chinatown, the Yengs were faced with one looming menace that surpassed other concerns such as the threat of bankruptcy or the hassles brought on by health inspectors with qualms about the way Peking duck was prepared. So far the Golden Pagoda had not been victimized by this certain menace, but Sam felt that it was only a matter of time before the inevitable occurred.

Sam was right.

It was just after sundown, and the evening crowd was filling up the dining room. Sam, his sleeves rolled up and an apron around his waist, roamed amongst the patrons, orchestrating business with his usual flair. He was not only owner, but also maitre d', waiter, busboy, and, when the orders started piling up, assistant chef. His daughter, Sun, and four other friends of the family made up the rest of his hard-working staff, and they had all collaborated for so long at the enterprise that they ran the restaurant as smoothly as other establishments with twice the manpower.

When a bell rang out over the kitchen door, Sam finished seating a couple at one of the window booths, then went to get the main courses that had been set out by the head chef. He deftly balanced two large trays on his taut, wiry arms, then made his way to the party of four at the far side of the room. Sun followed close behind him with a fresh pot of tea and pair of serving stands to set the trays on.

'Here we are,' Sam told the diners with a sincere smile as be began passing around the various offerings, which gave off a swirling variety of appetizing smells. 'Plates very hot, so be careful. Enjoy.'

Sun poured tea for the customers while they heaped compliments on her and her father for the service and quality of the food. 'Thank you,' she said modestly as she set the pot down at the end of the table. 'If you need anything else, just let us know.'

There was a sudden disturbance at the main entrance. The front door was kicked open with so much force that it was jarred from its hinges, and four men charged into the restaurant. They were dressed in black from head to toe, wearing ski masks to hide their features. All of them were carrying weapons, and the dining room soon filled with the deafening roar of gunfire. Ornate fixtures exploded, lights popped and went black, and mirrored panels shattered loudly above the terrified screams of the patrons.

'Everybody down!' one of the gunmen commanded. He was the largest of the four, an imposing figure with an unmistakable Chinese accent. He raked the tabletops with another volley from his machine gun, and the diners threw themselves to the floor in fear. Sam and his daughter were already on the carpet, lying close to one another.

'I knew they would come,' Sam whispered with anguished resignation. 'Why did it have to be when so many people are here?'

The leader of the men in black gave a signal for the others to hold their fire. In the wake of the fearcharged silence that followed, he walked across the room, kicking aside shards of broken china, and leaned over the restaurant's proprietor. When Sam refused to look at him, the man jabbed the butt of his rifle into Sam's ribs and grabbed him by a lock of hair to tilt his face up.

'You were given time!' the masked man shouted.

'I already told them,' Sam replied defiantly. 'I will not pay!'

'Stupid fool!' The leader shoved Sam roughly back to the floor, then strode over to the cash register, tipping over one of the tables on the way and forcing the patrons nearby to scramble on their knees to get out of the way of falling egg rolls and steaming chow mein. While the other gunmen kept their guns trained on the customers, he opened the register and began emptying its cash into a black bag he'd brought with him. Over his shoulder, he shouted at the patrons, 'Anyone who wants to leave this restaurant alive will put their wallets and jewelry on the floor in front of them! Now!'

As an added incentive, one of the armed men vented another round of gunfire in the direction of the bar, destroying a row of liquor bottles. Not about to call the men's bluff, the majority of those in the dining room quickly removed their wallets, purses, rings and watches and set them out in open view. The few that hesitated found a gunman soon at their side to give them a rough hand in contributing to the kitty. There were children in the restaurant, and their muted whimperings mixed with the outright screams of several babies to drive a deeper wedge of tension into the air. One man with heroic aspirations tried to trip one of the gunmen as he was walking by him and was rewarded with a blow to the side of the head that rendered him unconscious.

'Anyone else want to play games?' the man chortled viciously at those around him.

Once the loot had been gathered together by the four gunmen, their leader went back over to Sam and advised him, 'This is only a start. The Lung Chin says from now on you pay like everybody else. Tomorrow at two we'll be back. Then, every Tuesday after that the Lung Chin gets one thousand. Understood?'

Sam Yeng stared up at his tormentor, his eyes filled

with hate. 'You cannot do this!' he said.

The masked man laughed harshly, 'We already have! We can do more, too! Just watch!' He took a pack of matches from one of the tables and held it over a candle until all the matches had simultaneously ignited. Then he tossed the small makeshift torch over the counter of the bar. There was an explosion of flame as the spilled liquor spread the fire and began filling the room with smoke and triggering the smoke alarms and sprinkler system. Indignation overcame Sam and he struggled to his feet. The tall spokesman for the Lung Chin shoved Yeng against the nearest wall and held him there. 'And unless you can afford a bodyguard twenty-four hours a day for yourself and your beautiful daughter, you will not call the police!'

With a final series of gunblasts, the four intruders departed from the restaurant. Pandemonium erupted as the majority of the patrons rose to their feet and rushed for the side exit, leaving a few volunteers to help Sam and the other restaurant workers put out that portion of the blaze that had not been put out by the sprinklers. When the fire had been extinguished and the sprinklers shut down, Sam collapsed into the nearest chair, overcome by the import of everything that had just happened.

'Father,' Sun called out as she came to his side, 'Are you okay?'

Sam bobbed his head numbly, blinking back tears that were only partially due to the smoke that lingered in the air. He forced a sad, twisted smile and laughed with sad delirium, 'Our partners. . . they will not like this at all. . .'

The men he was speaking about were, at that moment, driving down the block towards the restaurant in the black van and sleek Corvette. Behind the wheel of the van, B.A. was the first to sense that something wasn't right.

'Hey, check out that station wagon, Hannibal!' he shouted, pointing at the vehicle parked in front of the Golden Pagoda. He had caught a glimpse of the last gunman slipping into the wagon. 'That guy had a rifle, man!'

The gangleader of the Lung China had already started

the engine, and before B.A. could act on his instincts, the station wagon lunged forward and sped past the van. B.A. was about to turn around to take up the pursuit when Hannibal saw the crowd pouring out of the restaurant and grabbed B.A.'s arm, saying, 'Hold it, I think we better check out the restaurant instead. We'll never catch those guys.'

B.A. pulled over to the kerb and Peck parked the Corvette behind the van. The A-Team got out and headed down the sidewalk toward the Golden Pagoda, just as Sam and Sun Yeng emerged. When the owners' grim gaze met the eyes of their silent partners, it was clear to the A-Team that there would be no feasting on Peking duck tonight. . .

SEVENTEEN

'Could be thousands, guys,' Peck said as the A-Team approached the entrance to the Golden Pagoda after Sam had told them what had happened. 'Brace yourselves.'

'If the damage is that bad, heads are gonna roll!' B.A. vowed. Once they'd stepped through the battered doorway, he saw that, if anything, Peck had underestimated the desecration. 'I can't believe this! They wrecked our restaurant, man!'

The smoke had subsided considerably, but its smell still choked the air and the acoustic ceiling had been shaded from its former white to a sootish grey. The sprinklers had soaked everything and the carpet squished underfoot as the Yengs led the A-Team through the dining room to survey the worst damage in the area of the bar and the surrounding walls. Hannibal could only shake his head at the sight. Peck was already juggling figures in his head, trying to come up with a rough estimate of the toll. Murdock stood off to one side, his hands tucked into his pocket and the fedora still cocked on his head. He plucked a swizzle stick from a nearby table and set it between his lips like a cigarette.

'The joint was a mess,' he intoned between imaginary puffs of the swizzle stick. 'It looked like we'd shown up too late for a demonstration of the world's biggest blender.'

'Damn,' Hannibal muttered, helping Sam to upright

one of the tables. 'We put away one pack of cockroaches and another batch crawls out of the woodwork.'

'Hannibal, do you think maybe somebody got wind we had a slice of the profits here and decided to hit the place to get back at us for putting Tillis and his goons on ice?'

Hannibal looked at Peck and shook his head. 'If somebody knew we had ties here and wanted to get back at us, they would have just waited for us to show up. No, I think we're dealing with something else here.' When he noticed Sam rubbing his shoulder, Hannibal asked him, 'Hey, are you okay?'

'Just a bruise,' Sam said. 'I be all right.'

'How about everyone else? Any other injuries?'

'They knocked one man out,' Sun Yen said, 'but he came to and left right away. Other than that, there was just a few cuts. Nothing serious.'

'Thank goodness for small favours,' Hannibal said.

'We got lucky I guess,' Yeng mused sadly.

'Lucky?' Peck scoffed, inspecting the singed drapes behind the bar. 'Look at this. They even wrecked the lace curtains. I loved these lace curtains! And the crystal! Hannibal, do you remember how hard it was to get some of this crystal from that distributor in New Orleans? I practically had to marry her.'

B.A. spotted a small pocket of flame about to spread across the tabletop next to him. He quickly grabbed a pot of tea and poured it over the fire until it was out. 'We own ten percent of a whole lotta nothin', man,' he groused, pounding his fist on the bar. 'Somebody's gonna pay! I'm gonna find out who did it and I'm gonna break their face!'

Sam and Sun had become overly quiet, distancing themselves from the A-Team as they helped their fellow workers begin the long task of cleaning up after the assault. Hannibal and Peck traded glances, then walked over to the Yengs. Murdock followed close behind.

'Who was it that did this, Sam?' Peck asked. 'We have a right to know. We're part owners of this place, too, remember.'

Sam Yeng was not a drinking man, but he reached

behind the bar and poured himself a finger's worth of sake from a bottle that had been spared the bullets of the gunmen. He drained the warm rice liquor in one long swallow, then eyed the A-Team forlornly and muttered, 'Lung Chin.'

'*The* Lung Chin?' Peck asked, already knowing the answer.

'Lung Chin,' Murdock drawled, 'sure, I knew the name. It rhymed with murder. Old Tong Family, one of the strongest in this whole sunbaked town. The big leagues. They were veterans at crime when Capone was still in nappies. Lung Chin. Yeah, we'd bit off a big one, all right.'

'What's with Murdock?' Hannibal asked. 'Is he late for his medication or something?'

'It's the hat,' Peck explained. 'He put it on back at the site and he's been the ghost of Sam Spade ever since.'

'This is gonna be worse than his dog bit,' B.A. predicted.

Murdock ignored the jibes and dropped his swizzle stick to the carpet, then ground it out under heel. Under his breath, he whispered, 'My partners were in a bad mood and threw a lot of lip my way. I tried to ignore it, but I found myself longing for the old days, when I worked alone out of walkup on Broadway and Seventh. Ah, the old days! There were times when I wanted to just crawl in a calendar and never come back.'

'Any time you wanna do that is fine with me, sucker!' B.A. said.

'Hannibal, what are we gonna do about this mess?' Peck asked.

'We take care of it,' Sam said. 'Not your problem.'

'Not our problem nothing,' Hannibal countered. 'Look, Sam, I don't know how you got on this Lung Chin's hit list, but they picked the wrong place to bust up. Nobody messes with our property or our friends.

Sam smiled appreciatively but insisted, 'This brought on by me. It is my problem to deal with.'

'Why'd they come after you, Sam?' Hannibal asked.

'You don't owe them money or anything like that, do you?'

Sam hesitated. His daughter came over and stood next to him. 'He doesn't owe them a thing. They want protection money and he refuses to pay it.' She put an arm around Sam and hugged him gently. 'My father is very brave and very proud but he needs your help.'

'Sun!' Sam interrupted angrily. 'Go help the others! This is my business!'

'No, I can't!' Sun told Hannibal and the others, 'My father wanted me to stay silent, but I can't stand back and let this go on. The Lung Chin will come back tomorrow and take the protection money from us and our customers until we have nothing! They have done it to others who tried to stand up to them. They have no mercy.'

'Sun!' Sam cut in again. 'This is for the men to decide!'

'Oh, dad, be serious!' Sun scolded. 'This isn't the twelfth century any more. The Lung Chin have guns, bullets, and cars, not just swords. You can't expect to stand up to them on your own. And besides, I've got a stake in this, too, remember. I have shares in this place and, more important, I have a dear father I don't want to lose because of his stubbornness.'

'You're outnumbered, Sam,' Hannibal said. 'The stock-holders have voted and we all agree that your problems are ours.

'I give you ten percent of the Golden Pagoda because you save my daughter from Viet Cong,' Sam told the A-Team. 'I owe *you*. It was a matter of honour. I was proud to do it.'

'Then you should understand it's a matter of honour to us not to let you face this alone,' Hannibal maintained.

'Terrible idea,' Sam said. 'You cannot fight Lung Chin with only four of you.'

'Yeah,' B.A. growled, 'it might not be fair if we hit 'em all at once, right, Hannibal?'

The A-Team shared a brief laugh, recalling a similar putdown they'd thrown in Crazy Tommy Tillis' face before they'd proceeded to disable his army of goons.

'Not a joke,' Sam said gravely. 'Lung Chin more dangerous than you know.'

'He's right,' Sun Yen said. Gesturing to the destruction around them, she continued, 'This was done by just four men. That is only a fraction of their power. The Lung Chin headquarters takes up an entire block less than a couple of miles from here, and it's a fortress. No one can go there unless they are invited.'

'Two hundred men!' Sam amplified, his anger unleashed by the sake. 'Two hundred strong, trained, and armed men. . . people in every doorway, every window. . . impossible to fight them in their grounds. . . They are killers. They take and take and take!'

'Easy, father.'

But Sam had lost his calm reserve. He clenched his small fists and shook them in the air as he glared at his daughter. 'All start with Tommy Chen!' he shouted. 'He responsible for this war on my family business!'

'He had nothing to do with what happened here!' Sun protested.

'Everything!' Sam shot back.

'Hey, hey, you two,' Hannibal said, stepping between the Yengs. 'What's going on here? Tommy Chen. . . isn't he your fiancé, Sun?'

'Was,' Sun corrected. Her secret sorrow rose to the surface and she was silent a few seconds as she fought back tears. When she had herself under control, she resumed, 'His father owed the Lung Chin and his father couldn't pay them. If Tommy hadn't joined, they would have killed his parents.'

'Tommy joined the Lung Chin?' Peck said.

'He didn't want to, I'm telling you! He had no choice!'

'No difference!' Sam claimed. 'He join and Lung Chin tell him to help make Sam Yeng pay. He come with those who destroy my restaurant.'

'That's not true, father! He wasn't one of the men who came here!'

'He never love you! He just a coward!'

'No! It's not true! He only broke the engagement

111

because he was ashamed.' Sun appealed to Hannibal, 'Maybe you can talk some sense into my father. He won't listen to me. I'm telling you, it wasn't Tommy's fault!'

Sun turned and ran off to the kitchen, burying her face in her hands. There was an uncomfortable moment of silence in the dining room as the A-Team waited for a reaction from Sam, who stood trembling before them, wrestling with some inner torment.

'I hurt my daughter's feelings,' he finally said, his voice tinged with guilt. 'I must go back and make up. We all talk later.'

'Sure thing, Sam.' Hannibal waited until the owner had left the dining room, then shook his head and told his partners, 'Looks like the Lung Chin breaks up more than restaurants. I want to close these bastards down and I want to do it fast.'

Peck had been scrawling down figures on a small note pad. He added them up and whistled at the total. 'There's at least eleven grand in damage here. Ten percent of that is eleven hundred. . . divided by four. . . comes to two hundred and seventy five bucks apiece from us, Hannibal. Of course, I think there'll be some insurance coverage for part of this.'

'Right, I'm sure Sam's got a clause to protect him against Tong wars,' Hannibal said cynically.'

'Well, I say we collect from the guys that did this,' B.A. suggested. 'Right now!'

Murdock slipped an egg roll into his mouth and chewed it down, then wiped his lips with a napkin and popped another swizzle stick in his mouth before slipping back into character. 'The one who called himself the Colonel was looking to clean his shoes on somebody's mug,' he narrated to himself. 'I decided it was worth taggin' along.'

'Wherever we end up goin',' B.A. said, 'I hope we go by the vet's hospital on the way so we can drop this nutbar off. I can't take any more of his jive, man!'

'Murdock, you stay with Face in the 'vette,' Hannibal ordered. 'I think we ought to get a good night's sleep and start out on this thing fresh in the morning.'

'It was time for winks,' Murdock said. 'I was ready to count forty of them.'

B.A. waved a fist in Murdock's face. 'You're gonna be countin' stars before I'm done with you, fool!'

EIGHTEEN

Night winds had cleared away most of the smog in the city basin, and the next morning the skies were crisp and blue. The morning sun shone brightly on Chinatown, infusing the architectural reds and greens with a vibrant glow. Sculpted dragons snarled before doorways and from within alcoves and other niches in the buildings that lined the streets, their expressions in sharp contrast with those of the scattered happy Buddhas who beamed their well-being in the midst of small, cloistered gardens lush with coloured blossoms and groomed bonsai trees. Kitchens were heating up for the day, and the aroma of spices and exotic herbs spilled out into alleys and carried to the streets, where they mingled with the noxious fumes of mid-morning traffic. It was too early in the day for tourists; the majority of those using the streets and sidewalks were Asian-Americans who lived and worked in the area. Some still wore the garb of their oriental ancestors, but more common was Western dress that reflected the tastes of their new homes. The predominant buzz of conversation, however, remained Chinese, with its quick, choppy rhythms.

The A-Team drove slowly down the street in B.A.'s van, feeling the scrutiny that was being focused on them.

'Maybe we should have come in a rickshaw with your dressed as Mr Lee,' Peck told Hannibal as they waited at an intersection for the lights to change. 'Then at least one of us wouldn't be sticking out like a sore thumb.'

'I think if they can sniff out Charlie Chan as a phony, they'd have no trouble seeing through Mr Lee.' Hannibal puffed on his cigar and tapped ash out into the street as they drove on. 'Sam said the headquarters are at the end of this next block, didn't he?'

Peck checked the street numbers on the corner grocery against those on a slip of paper in his hand. 'Yeah, we're about there, Hannibal.'

'Won't be too soon for me,' B.A. said, gripping the steering wheel hard. 'I got a feeling some of these dudes are lookin' at us with more than curiosity.'

Murdock leaned forward and peered out the windshield from under the brim of his fedora. 'Yeah, we were being watched all right, to put it mildly,' he said. 'We had more eyes on us that a truckload of spuds. Mean eyes, too. The kind of eyes that would raise the hackles of any God-fearing man –'

'Murdock, shut up!' B.A. reached out and stiff-armed Murdock, sending him sprawling back to the rear of the van with Peck.

Murdock picked up his fallen fedora and propped it back on his head as he stuck his tongue out at B.A. and stuffed his hands into the pockets of his coat. Peck kept staring out the side window, not liking what he saw. 'Seems to me half the people out there are Lung Chin heavies doing sentry duty. I get this funny feeling we aren't going to get much closer to their headquarters without being stopped.'

'He's right man,' B.A. said. 'Somethin' big's gettin' ready to go down here.'

Peck speculated, 'Could be they're bracing to make a move on Crazy Tommy T's turf. I mean, they can't be expecting us. . . can they?'

'Nah,' Hannibal said. 'Don't worry. We're just taking an innocent, slow little drive down the street.'

'Sure we were,' Murdock whispered into the raised collar of his jacket, 'but somewhere around this pagoda factory something seemed to be closing in on me. Yeah, something big, all right, something we maybe wouldn't find. Something that had been ringing a lot of gongs from one end of my gut to the other.

'I'll ring your gong for good, sucker!' B.A. shouted, glaring at Murdock in the rear-view mirror.

But Murdock was caught up in his newfound persona, marching to the tune of a different saxophone that blew smoky notes somewhere deep inside his mind. 'No matter how much cologne I splashed on it, there was no getting around one basic fact.' He paused significantly, as if waiting for an unseen camera to zoom in for a tight close-up on his face. 'This whole caper had Mack Murdock trackin' the hoofprints of that most elusive of all maguffins – The Maltese Cow!'

'The Maltese what?' Peck muttered.

B.A. stopped for traffic and turned around in his seat. 'I said lose it, fool!' he admonished Murdock. 'You ain't Mack Murdock. You're just crazy! And from now on you're gonna be crazy quiet, got it? Not a word!'

'Fellas, how about if we save the sparring for later?' Hannibal said. 'We're coming up on our target, unless I miss my guess.'

Toward the end of the block, small stores dwindled and were replaced by larger buildings and warehouses. At the far corner, a single monolith of brick and steel loomed over an entire block. Hannibal leaned forward slightly in his seat to get a better look at the building, and something on the upper level caught his eye.

'Second floor on your right, guys,' he said.

The others looked up in time to see a hand pulling a set of drapes shut behind the upper window Hannibal had mentioned.

'Got it,' Peck said.

'And in the doorway across the street,' Hannibal said, pointing to a figure lurking in the shadows. Before the others could get a good look at him, he shrank back from view. 'Pretty good magic act.'

'I just hope we don't end up disappearing as fast as they do,' Peck said. 'They might not know who we are, but I get this feeling that it's strangers in general they don't care much for.'

As B.A. drove through the next intersection, Hannibal noted that there were suspicious-looking cars parked at all corners, filled with even more suspicious-looking men.

'I felt as if we had blundered into a samurai convention,' Murdock said. 'I hoped they'd left their swords at home, because if they lost their cool, anybody who stood in their way would end up looking like something that had been through a Veg-o-matic.'

'Swords nothing,' Peck muttered. 'It's another kinda steel I'm worried about them toting.'

'You can bet on them having guns.' B.A. said. 'A lot more of 'em than we have, too.'

The van slowed down as they passed the large building. There seemed to be only one entrance, and it was guarded by a band of six men, each one the size of B.A., standing cross-armed and glaring defiantly at the A-Team.

'Quite a complaints department,' Peck said. 'Makes you think twice about coming around looking for refunds. I don't know about you, Hannibal, but I'm sorta willing to write off my share of the damages.

'We're just going to have to be a little creative, that's all.' Hannibal put his cigar out, then told B.A., 'Let's go around the corner and see what our buddies do when we change direction.'

'Okay, but I can already tell you what they're gonna do.' B.A. said, making the turn. 'They're onto us like glue, man!'

Although the men guarding the entrance to the Lung Chin headquarters stayed put, there were others lurking about to take up the surveillance of the A-Team.

'Everywhere I turned, I saw eyes watching me,' Murdock said. 'It was like Hitchcock directing 'The Birds' with an all-Tong cast. They were everywhere, just waiting for the right moment.'

B.A. drove slowly down the side street. In the back of the van, Peck quietly opened the footlocker containing the A-Team's trove of weapons. He passed around guns to all the men.

'Keep 'em hidden,' Hannibal said, slipping his revolver under his coat. 'The last thing we want to do is provoke anything. That comes later, once my plan starts falling into place.'

'You got a plan?' B.A. said.

'I always have a plan,' Hannibal replied. 'You know that.'

'Well, what's it now?'

'Wait-and-see.'

'Some plan,' B.A. mumbled. 'I bet even Murdock coulda come up with that.'

'B.A., watch out!' Peck suddenly shouted.

B.A. pumped the brakes and the van skidded to a halt just as a long, cherry-red limousine abruptly shot in front of them from a side alley. In the back of the limo was an old, withered man with a wisp of hair dripping from his chin. He stared out the window at the van, his face devoid of expression, an enigmatic cipher. Peck hurriedly snatched up his camera and managed to take a quick shot of the man before the limo glided past and was swallowed by the large building, which had thrown open an automatic garage door like the upper jaws of a great beast.

'Hmmmm,' Hannibal said as the door closed on the garage. 'I think we were just treated to a view of the Lung Chin's top banana. What's his name?'

'Wan Chu,' Peck said.

'He sounded like someone who went well with plum sauce,' Murdock remarked. 'But the look of the goons he travelled with didn't do anything for my appetite.'

Before the van could pick up speed, four black sedans screeched into view from different directions and boxed the A-Team in. Doors started opening, and musclebound thugs piled out. One of them, who vaguely resembled James Bond's old rival, Odd Job, walked purposefully toward the van.

'I think maybe we saw something we weren't supposed to,' Hannibal said. 'Everybody be calm. No guns unless we need 'em.'

When the Chinese giant stopped next to Hannibal's side of the van, Hannibal rolled down his window.

'You're lost,' the giant said coldly.

'Actually, we're just taking a little spin,' Hannibal said. He could tell the story wasn't washing and tried to change the subject. 'The old boy in the limo must be a big shot of some kind, huh? Rock star maybe?'

'You're someplace you shouldn't be,' the other man responded, peering past Hannibal at the rest of the Team. 'You cops?'

'How'd ya know?' Peck chirped, holding his camera behind his back and his gun behind Hannibal's seat. 'We were just wondering if you wanted to buy tickets to the Policeman's Ball next month.'

'You're not cops. I think you better move on before something happens to your van. It's a rough neighbourhood here.'

'So I noticed,' Hannibal said, eyeing the thugs who were standing next to the other cars.

'How do you expect us to move when you got my wheels trapped here, sucker!?' B.A. challenged.

'B.A.' Hannibal gestured for him to cool it, then smiled apologetically at the man outside the van. 'My friends here are just teasing you because they can see you have a sense of humour. Truth is, we're amateur spinners.'

'What?'

'You know, people who take a spin.' Hannibal reached for his wallet. 'If you want, I'll show you my card. I head up the west coast chapter. We've been expanding like crazy the past few years. Maybe you saw the write-up we got in the last issue of Rolling –'

'Leave,' the giant said, refusing to look at Hannibal's wallet. 'Now.' He raised a hand and snapped his fingers. One of his cohorts got into the sedan that was blocking the van's front end and backed up, giving the A-Team room to move on. 'And don't come back if you know what's good for you.'

'Excuse me,' Hannibal said as he put his wallet away. 'Maybe I'm just confused, but isn't this Los Angeles,

California? United States of America? Where men can take a spin down the street if they feel like it because it's a free country and we've got a right to?'

'You got the right,' the man conceded. 'You might not have arms to hold the wheel, though. Your choice.'

Hannibal grinned. 'Like I was saying, we'll just be on our way. Nice place you have here.'

The giant stared back at Hannibal with icy silence. Hannibal rolled up his window as B.A. drove past the other thugs. Some of them got into one of the cars and started following the A-Team.

'Friendly folks,' Peck commented. 'We want to make sure we don't get lost again.'

'Yeah, well I hope they don't follow us too far,' B.A. said.

'I don't think they will,' Hannibal said. 'They just don't want anyone on their turf.'

Sure enough, two blocks further down the street, the sedan turned off into an alley, leaving the van to proceed on its own.

'Hannibal, it'd take an army to get in that place back there,' B.A. complained.

'We'll worry about that later.' Hannibal checked his watch. 'Right now I think we ought to get back to Sam's. Remember, he's expecting visitors at two. Maybe we'll get to meet some of our new friends there. I sure hope so. I think one good show of hospitality deserves another.'

'You got a plan for that, too?' B.A. said cynically. 'Or are we gonna "wait-and-see" again?'

'Oh, I was thinking we'd try to expand their cultural horizons when they show up,' Hannibal said. 'I bet they'd get a real kick out of some jazz. . .'

120

NINETEEN

The hourly gong at China Savings had already sounded twice when the Lung Chin sedan rolled down the street and slid into a parking space in front of the Golden Pagoda. The men inside glanced at one another to assure themselves they were all ready for their raid, then pulled on their ski masks and donned black gloves. One of the men in the back withdrew the rug that had been concealing their weapons. After he'd passed around the guns, the four of them got out of the car and headed for the restaurant. The main door had been replaced, along with the hinges and jamb, and it was half opened, eliminating the necessity for them to kick it in. They pushed their way through the entrance, guns raised and ready to use. They had been expecting to find a fair share of late lunchers, but they discovered that the dining area had been left largely unrepaired and the only person in the entire room was Hannibal. He sat at a folding card table, calmly sipping tea as he munched on fried noodles. He glanced at the intruders over the top of his cup before lowering it and checking his watch.

'Guys, you're late,' he scolded with a wag of his finger. 'It's five past two already. You shouldn't have stopped for burgers on the way. Fast food isn't as fast as it used to be, you know.'

The four gang members stepped further into the dining room and lowered their guns as they looked around. Their

121

leader asked Hannibal, 'Where is everyone else?'

Hannibal shrugged. 'Beats me. Maybe it has something to do with the new interior decorating. Not much of a punk clientele in these parts, I guess.'

'I'm talking about the old man,' the gunman retorted. 'He owes us money. Where's Sam Yeng?'

'He went hang-gliding,' Hannibal explained, fidgeting with a fresh cigar before popping it in his mouth. 'He left a message for me to give to you, though. He says you're a little confused about who owes who what. The way I understand it, you were supposed to be dropping by to pay for these damages from your rough-housing yesterday. Look, I know how it is with you rock-and-roll bands. . . always tearing up hotel rooms and then having your accounts settle the tab –'

'We are not a rock-and-roll band!' the leader shouted. 'We are Lung Chin, and we come for what Sam Yeng owes us. If you will not get it for us, we will get it for ourselves.'

As the lead gunman strode over to the cash register, Hannibal lit his cigar, then drawled, 'You know, I have to tell you that's not gonna sit too well with my buddies.'

'What buddies?' another of the intruders asked.

'This one for starters, sucker!' B.A. shouted out as he appeared from a closet near the lobby and shut the front door. He had an M-16, too, and when the masked men moved to take aim at him, he spat lead at them and shouted, 'Drop your guns or I'm gonna drop *you*!'

Hannibal retrieved a revolver from under his napkin and seconded B.A.'s warning. As if the Lung Chin needed any more convincing, Peck emerged from the kitchen with a submachine gun and Mack Murdock popped up behind the bar with an old .45 with new bullets.

'This place is messy enough, sweetheart,' Murdock told the Lung Chin as he tapped back the brim of his fedora. 'You don't want to make us mess it up any more. Be nice and we'll just use you for mops.'

'Hey, Murdock,' B.A. confessed, 'That was a good one! Now how about quittin' while you're ahead!?'

The gang leader tossed his gun to the carpet and his followers did the same. His other hand was still poised over the cash register.

'Go ahead,' Hannibal told him. 'Open it!'

The gangleader hesitated.

'You didn't suddenly forget your English, did you?' Peck asked. 'He told you to open it.'

The masked man pressed the 'no sale' button and the cash drawer opened up. There was no cash inside, though. A scrap of paper read: 'U.O.US 50 GRAND.'

'That stands for "You owe us", in case you hadn't figured,' Hannibal said. 'The fifty Gs is just an estimate until we get our hands on the robbery report from the police and figure out how much you lifted from the diners yesterday. Tell your boss if he pays up and promises to keep away from the Golden Pagoda, we won't bother with punitive damages.'

One of the other gang members had brought along a makeshift, portable firebomb. It was clipped to his belt, and while the A-Team was distracted elsewhere, he managed to get his hands on the bomb and pull its triggering pin. He lobbed it behind the bar, then dived to the floor.

'Oh, you dirty rat!' Murdock howled, seeing the bomb roll out of reach under the bar. He frantically leapt away from the bar, in the same motion tackling the man who had thrown the bomb and was now trying to make a run for it. The bomb didn't explode, but it did begin to give off a billowing cloud of smoke. Taking advantage of the disruption, the other three members of the Lung Chin sprang forward and lashed out with martial art kicks, disarming Hanibal, B.A., and Peck and beginning a free-for-all brawl. In hand-to-hand combat, the two sides were evenly matched. B.A. took a few karate chops without budging, then managed to get a good grip on his opponent's wrists. With a discus-thrower's delivery, he slung the man over the top of the bar and into the midst of the smoke. Peck duelled his foe with chairs, trading awkward swipes and ripostes, the two of them looking something like fencers trying to joust underwater. The other man was slightly stronger than Peck and managed to back him up as far as the juke-box. When the chair came crashing down on him, Peck dodged to one side at the last second and the glass facing shattered. Peck grabbed a couple of the records and whipped them like diet frisbees. His attacker screamed as the platters bit into his arms, which he'd thrown in front of his face. Peck followed through with a right cross that had served him well in the past. His fist caught the other man by surprise and he collapsed at Peck's feet. Hannibal relied on his own expertise at martial arts and managed to beat the gang leader at his own game. As the cloud of smoke filled out the room, the victorious A-Team grabbed its victims and hauled them off to the kitchen. As Murdock went back out to the dining room to retrieve the weapons, he chortled to himself, 'The Lung Chin boys were spilled across the floor like spilled milk. We weren't going to cry over them though. . . no, too redundant. . . The Lung Chin were spilled over the floor like a six-pack of cheap liquor. . . nah, too trite. . . gotta have something snazzier.'

Along with the guns, he fetched his fallen hat and put it back on. The fedora brought him inspiration, and after several more reworkings, he stumbled on a metaphor that satisfied him. He marched back into the kitchen with a sniggering grin.

'You okay, Murdock?' Hannibal asked him. 'Looks like you got your jaw knocked out of place.'

'Just a scratch,' Murdock replied. 'Small price to pay for a chance to spill those Lung Chin across the floor like a six-pack of broken promises. . .'

'Hannibal,' B.A. pleaded as he grabbed the machine gun from Murdock and held it on the gang members, 'tell this fool to shut up!'

'Murdock, give it a rest,' Hannibal said, pinching his cigar together where it had become cracked during the fighting. 'Besides, there's only four of them here, not six.'

'Yeah, but what kind of image is a four-pack?' Murdock whined.

While his partners kept an eye on the Lung Chin, Hannibal started pacing the kitchen, idly fingering the cooking utensils, lost in thought.

'I take it this is only stage one of your plan,' Peck told Hannibal. 'You're not saying anything. . . that means you're spinning a web in there.'

Hannibal's mental light bulb lit up and he grinned. 'No big thing, Face. I think we'll indulge ourselves in a wardrobe change, then maybe go on a visit, maybe back to these yoyos' headquarters. Only this time we get inside.'

'Inside?' B.A. scoffed, 'You gotta be dreamin', Hannibal!'

Hannibal shook his head, still riding out his train of thought. 'And once we get inside, things are going to heat up faster than. . . than a cheap car in the middle of July. How's that, Murdock?'

'There was no dodgin' it,' Murdock deadpanned, happy to be unleashed again, 'the Colonel knew a catchy image when he heard one. But maybe that's the difference between a colonel and a side of hash browns, when you think about it.'

B.A. gave up his protests and shook his head with disgust as he kept the gun trained on the four masked men. Hannibal went over to their leader and tugged the ski mask off his head. 'How's it going, friend? You started to feel like you made a bad career move about now?'

The man pressed his lips tightly together and looked away.

'What's this?' Peck said. 'Not even a name, rank, and serial number? Didn't Wan Chu teach you guys any prisoner etiquette?'

Hannibal held his opened palm out in front of the unmasked man. 'Let's have your car keys.'

When the gangster acted as if he hadn't heard, Hannibal took Murdock's old revolver and cocked the hammer, then pressed the cold steel of the barrel against the prisoner's forehead.

'Okay,' the man finally whispered hoarsely, his face red

with fury and shame.

Hannibal pulled the gun away and let the man reach to his pocket for a ring of keys. Hannibal took them and sorted through until he found the one he was looking for. 'Peck, take this key out and see if it fits in that sedan these gentlemen came here in. If it is, I think we'll have found our ticket into the Lung Chin's mystery condo.'

'Hannibal, do you really think anyone's going to buy us as Tongs?'

'They don't have to buy,' Hannibal said, 'They only have to rent. But, before we get into any of that, there's somebody I want to meet with.'

'Who's that?' Peck asked.

'Honestly, Face, I'd have thought that by now you'd know that the chief element in my plans is the element of surprise.'

'Yeah, but not when the surprise ends up being on us.'

'Well, let me put it this way,' Hannibal responded. 'I've always wanted to try my hand at marriage counselling. . .'

TWENTY

For the second time that day, the A-Team ventured into the heart of Chinatown. The tourists were out in full force now, clicking their way through rolls of film that would eventually be developed into slides that would torment trapped relatives who weren't particularly interested in seeing their kin gaping at the camera with their arms around stone gargoyles, rotund Buddhas, pigeon-pelted dragons or anything else that had the misfortune to be within squeezing range. The souvenir shops were doing the briskest business, peddling wares that ranged from bagged fortune cookies to silk kimonos to oriental whoopie cushions and three-dimensional postcards of Geisha girls who winked at you if you looked at them the right way. A sizeable crowd was gathered around one of the more authentic-looking storefronts, where a movie crew was filming a rock video in which a British synthesizer band mouth-synched the words to their latest hit while they stood under oriental arches and were caressed by women who looked like models for the Peking outlet of Frederick's of Hollywood.

'Hey, B.A., I bet you'd fit right into their film,' Peck said, staring out the window of the van. 'Put a whip in your hand and paint one of your teeth gold and you'd put Michael Jackson out of business in a week, I guarantee it.'

'Funny man,' B.A. grumbled as he drove by. He continued a few blocks past the major concentration of tourist traps, then slowed down as Hannibal and Peck scrutinized the storefronts operated by the tradesmen of the area. There were bakeries, garment shops, craft stores, and numerous laundry establishments. It was finally Murdock who spotted the place they were looking for.

'There it was,' he droned. 'Chen's Laundry. You mess 'em, we press 'em. Most people let off steam once they're out of work; at Chen's letting off steam was what paid the bills. I had some problems that needed ironing, and I was hoping Chen would be able to help without giving me the runaround the collar –'

B.A. wriggled the van into a parking space, then turned off the ignition and bolted into the back seat. He pinned Murdock to the carpet and demanded, 'I wanna hear you say something that don't sound like it's comin' out of an old movie!' He grabbed Murdock's fedora and threatened to rip off the brim. 'Come on, fool, let's hear it!'

Murdock laughed uneasily as he stared up at his wary ally. 'Hey, B.A., at least I didn't bring Billy along to try to sniff out some clues. Right?'

Hannibal got out of the van and called over his shoulder, 'Face and I are going in. If you two cubs want to wrestle back there, fine. Just make sure you kiss and make up before we come back.'

Peck joined Hannibal on the sidewalk, but before he reached the entrance to the laundry, he spotted a young woman puzzling over a map in front of the next storefront down. She had longer legs than last summer's blockbuster and reeked of the kind of vulnerability that registered in Peck's brain like the most powerful of aphrodisiacs.

'Listen, Hannibal,' he said, patting his partner on the back. 'You don't need me to handle this one. Why don't I give you room to move, okay?'

Hannibal looked past Peck at the woman. 'I think you're the one looking for room to move, Face. Okay, if I need you, I'll. . . probably be out of luck.'

'I knew you'd understand,' Peck said. 'I'll keep an eye open for Sun and send her in as soon as she gets here.'

Hannibal watched Peck wander over to the woman, then turned and headed into the laundry, mumbling to himself, 'That's what I like about this team. . . we're such a cohesive unit.

Inside the small laundry, there was only one person working, a young man who was labouring before a large steam press. His sleeves were rolled up and he was sweating from both the pace of his work and the wet mist that clung around him like a low-hanging cloud every time he pumped the press. He was surrounded by clothes on hangers, and there was a slight smile on his face because after hours of toil he'd reached the point where the work completed was far greater than that needed to be done. He hummed to himself, absorbed in his work. He didn't see Hannibal enter the shop. Hannibal quickly stole to one side of the store and slipped under the swinging portion of the counter. He was dressed in black, wearing the outfit of the Lung Chin ringleader the A-Team had left handcuffed with his associates to a large gong located behind one of the bigger import shops in Chinatown. In their underwear, the former terrorists had struck far-from-imposing figures as they were left to be discovered by the Tong affiliates that ran the shop. Hannibal had taken all the man's outfit, including the black gloves and the wristband with the stamped insignia that identified him as a bonafide member of the Lung Chin. He was already wearing the wristband, and he donned the gloves as he weaved his way through the starched shirts and pressed pants towards the sweating worker. When he was less than two feet away, Hannibal reached out and grabbed the man's shoulder, spinning him around.

'Tommy Chen?' Hannibal asked.

Chen stared at Hannibal, quaking with fear. He nodded, then couldn't stop bobbing his head up and down. 'Wh. . . wh. . . who are y. . . y. . . you?' he stammered.

'I don't know,' Hannibal said. 'Maybe I'm your conscience. Maybe I'm the Ghost of Marriage Past. . .'

Chen grabbed his chin and succeeded in stilling his

head. He took a deep breath, then reached behind him for a hand iron, which he held in his cocked arm as if he meant to use it as an oversized set of brass knuckles. 'Whoever you are, you've no business here,' he managed to say without his voice warbling on him. 'Don't force me to hit you.'

There was a sudden voice from the front of the store. 'He's my friend.' It was Sun Yeng. She stepped forward, pointing at the iron in Chen's hand. 'Put that down, Tommy. You've got to help us.'

Chen stared with confusion at Sun Yeng, slowly lowering the iron. He offered no resistance when Hannibal reached out and took it from him. 'It's not possible,' he muttered feebly, looking away from his former fiancé. 'I cannot help you. It can't be done.'

'Sure it can, Tommy,' Hannibal assured him. 'All we wanna know is what's going on around here.'

'Where?'

'All around the back streets of Chinatown, Tommy. Off the beaten track, where there's enough muscle guarding the Lung Chin headquarters to overthrow some countries.' Hannibal pulled the gloves off and continued, 'Now, we know if can't look like that all the time, so we figure there's something bigger than a breadbox going on. You want to fill us in?'

'I don't talk to cops!' Chen's confidence was blooming by the second now that he'd overcome his initial surprise. He glared at Sun and demanded, 'How can you bring him here?'

'He's not a cop,' Sun insisted. 'You have to trust me.'

Just then the door to the laundry opened again, and the rest of the A-Team entered, each of them dressed in black, save for Murdock's brown fedora. B.A.'s outfit was several sizes too small for him, and he threatened to burst it at the seams with each movement he made. Peck smiled briefly at Hannibal and said, 'She found her way once I turned her map rightside up. She didn't want me to come along for the ride, so I thought I'd let these guys out of their cage and join the party.'

'Party?' Chen was having trouble following what was happening. 'There's no party here.'

'Just a figure of speech, Tommy,' Hannibal said, 'Something along the lines of "You have nothing to fear but fear itself". Look, we know you didn't want to join the Lung Chin. Let us help you, Tommy. Maybe we can even work things out so you two can get back together.'

Chen and Sun looked at one another, exchanging between them a mutual anguish that had been brought upon them by the circumstances of the forced cancellation of their wedding. Chen's anger faded by the time he looked back at Hannibal. 'What about my folks?' he said. 'They'll be in a lot of danger. That's the whole reason I'm doing –'

'If you're worried about them,' Hannibal advised, 'close the place down and take a vacation with them. By the time you get back, we can have the neighbourhood holding its head up again. That's the best we can do, but you gotta meet us halfway.'

'I don't know,' Chen said, groping with the proposition. 'It isn't that simple to me. . .'

'Do like Hannibal says,' B.A. told the young man. 'It's a whole lot better than letting that club you're in walk all over your life.'

'I need some time to think about it,' Chen stalled.

Sun stepped forward and ducked under the counter, then came over and took her lover's hand, squeezing it tightly. 'Please, Tommy,' she pleaded. 'Listen to your heart. Do the right thing. . . for us. There's still hope for us, but you have to stand up for what you believe in.'

Chen squeezed Sun's hand back and let out his final reservations with a long exhalation of relief. 'There's a man named Chris Thomas coming in at four on an oil tanker,' he told Hannibal. 'Pier 52, down at the docks.'

'Oh, man,' B.A. winced, 'not the docks!'

'Chris Thomas.' Hannibal stared into space, running the name through his cerebral files until he came up with a cross-reference. 'I remember him now. . . he was the mobster who got deported about ten years back, right?'

'Yes! Yes, how did you know that?' Chen asked, impressed.

'My friends and I were cooling our heels in the stockade back then,' Hannibal said. 'We had lots of time to follow the papers. My guess is this Thomas has got homesick and now he wants to get back into the same line of business that got him booted out of the country back then. So far so good?'

'Your guess is as good as mine,' Chen confided. 'I don't know anything about him, and I figure the less I find out the better off I'm gonna be.'

'Well, you must have caught wind of something,' Hannibal said. 'Come on, Tommy, quite holding back. The more info you can give us, the better we're gonna be able to take the right action. That's the name of the game here.'

'Okay, okay,' Chen relented. 'The Lung Chin's giving this Thomas guy a new identity, new papers, everything. They're sneaking him back into the US and in return he's going to give them a slice of the drug operation he hopes to set up now that Tom Angel's in the slammer.'

'That was one of our jobs,' Peck told Chen. 'We put Angel behind bars, along with Crazy Tommy Tillis and his boys. . . so believe me, if anybody's going to take the Lung Chin head-on, it's us. So you want to back the winner all the way and be with us?'

'Yes,' Chen said. 'Just tell me what you want me to do and I'll do it.'

'I already told you,' Hannibal said. 'Be smart and vanish for a few days. Take your family with you. When this is all over, you and Sun Yeng will have a lot to talk about. And we'll owe you one, Tommy.'

Chen put his other hand over Sun's and held her tightly as he told the A-Team, 'Maybe I'll be the one who owes you.'

Standing near the door, Murdock muttered, 'The room was thick with gratitude. I wanted to take a knife and slice it, maybe stash some of the extra away in my refrigerator for a day when I needed it.'

TWENTY-ONE

'Well, this one'll get filed under "Trojan Horse Manoeuvres", don't you think, guys?'

Hannibal looked at the rest of the A-Team. They were in the Lung Chin sedan they'd taken from the heavies who had tried to give an encore demonstration of terrorism at the Golden Pagoda. They were still dressed in black, but they hadn't yet pulled down their ski masks to cover their features.

'Oh, I don't know about that, Hannibal,' Peck countered. 'I mean, we aren't exactly bearing gifts, not like that tequila truck number we pulled on those banditos down in Ecuador. I think this is more along the lines of "When in Rome, do as the Romans".'

'Whatever.'

In the back seat, Murdock was sitting as far away from B.A. as he could, the better to ramble on with his Bogart patter. 'Call it a fixation,' he whispered, 'but the Maltese Cow was haunting me, it's cryptic moo beckoning like the scent of a cheap USO dance hostess. . .'

B.A. turned to him. 'I'll break your nose and box your ears and you won't have to worry about hearin' or smellin' nothin', Murdock!'

'Cool it back there in the peanut gallery,' Hannibal said as he put out his cigar. 'We're almost there.'

They were travelling the same stretch of roadway they had earlier in the day, coming up on the Lung Chin headquarters. Hired thugs were still out in abundance, warding off tourists and anyone else who didn't have business in the area. Because they were in the sedan, the A-Team were able to advance without undue notice, although they made sure not to spend too much time looking out the side windows and risking the discovery that they weren't who they appeared to be.

'Yeah, we were almost there, all right,' Murdock said. 'The moo of the Maltese Cow filled my brain like a mantra.'

'Okay, masks down,' Hannibal ordered.

B.A. tugged his cap down over his face, then slapped the fedora off Murdock's head. 'You ain't wearin' that inside the joint, fool! Get your mask down. Maybe we'll be lucky and yours won't have a hole for your big mouth!'

As they rounded the corner near the main entrance, Peck took one hand off the steering wheel and bared his wrist for one of the guards in front of the building to see. He did it nonchalantly, not sure if it was necessary to flash the band with the Lung Chin insignia to pass. The guard gave a perfunctory wave of his hand and Peck drove on down the side street, approaching the garage where Wan Chu's limousine had vanished during their last trip this way.

'Okay, here goes nothing,' Peck said. 'Open sesame. . .'

As if on his cue, the metal door rolled open. Peck turned and drove the sedan through the opening and down the inclined driveway to an underground garage. Wan Chu's limousine was parked there, along with two other sedans similar to the one the A-Team was in. To their relief, the garage was not heavily guarded. The man who had opened the door was the only one there, and once he'd closed the door, he approached the sedan, not bothering to unsling the automatic rifle hanging from his shoulder.

'Yeng give you any flak?' he asked as the four men in black got out of the sedan.

Hannibal shook his head, avoiding the other man's gaze.

'He paid it all, then?' the rifleman asked.

B.A. moved around behind the guard, who narrowed his eyes in suspicion at the gargantuan frame of the imposter. 'Somebody paid,' B.A. said, lashing out with a hearty uppercut. The guards jaw snapped upward and his eyes went cloudy as he wilted into Peck's waiting arms. Murdock unslung the man's rifle and set it aside.

'You know, B.A., this guy looks to be more your size,' Hannibal remarked as he stared at the unconscious man before him. 'I think it'd be a good idea if you did another quick change before we go any further. The odds go up from here on.'

As B.A. was dragging the guard into a side alcove to swap clothes, Peck and Murdock strode over to the cherry red limo. Peck tried the door.

'Locked,' he muttered. 'I can pick it, but that'll take a little time, and I'm already going to need a while to do a good job of planting this bug.' He removed a small monitoring device the size of his palm.

Hannibal was standing near the inner door that connected the garage to the rest of the building. He suddenly turned away from the door and hissed at the others, 'Someone's coming!'

B.A. stayed huddled in the alcove while Peck and Murdock scrambled for cover behind the limousine. Seconds later, three Lung Chin members entered the garage and nodded absently at Hanibal, who pretended to be standing guard near the controls that operated the garage door. The gangsters piled into one of the other sedans, and Hannibal quickly figured out how to open the main door so that they could back out. Once the car was out of the building, he closed the door and let out a breath.

'Okay, gang. The coast is clear for now,' he said. 'Let's go for it.'

B.A. came out of the alcove, tucking in the black sweatshirt he'd taken off the unconscious guard. It was still small on him, but not as blatantly as his previous disguise. They took their guns out and paused a moment, then headed into the inner sanctum of the Lung Chin.

135

TWENTY-TWO

The main hallway of the Lung Chin headquarters was lavish beyond belief. Unlike much of the decoration that adorned Chinatown, the trappings here were not copies or cheap imitations of work done back in the motherland. They were the real thing, and they looked it. The vases on wooden pedestals were true Ming dynasty, and the tapestries on the walls were of pure silk. Centuries-old watercolours were framed in gold, and the plush rugs lining the polished teak floor had been made by the finest artisans in all of China

'Looks like a damn museum,' B.A. whispered as he and the others padded down the corridor.

'And decent folk like Sam Yeng paid for some of it with protection money, you can be sure of it,' Hannibal said as he led the Team past closed doors. Whenever they came to a crossway, the four of them would slow down to see if anyone was about. The passageway was oddly deserted, however.

'I don't get it,' Peck said, 'This place is crawling with guards on the outside, but in here it looks like nobody's home.'

'I get the feeling there's probably a big meeting going on somewhere in here,' Hannibal said. 'One of those mandatory attendance numbers. That might work in our favour.'

'Yeah,' B.A. murmured, 'instead of fightin' a lot of

136

little battles, we can take 'em all on at once. We'll probably be outnumbered twenty to one!'

'If that's the case,' Hannibal joked, 'we'll be sure to let them send out for some more guys to even up the odds, right?'

Murdock hung back from the others, giving a *film noir* play-by-play commentary. 'We'd crawled into the mouth of the great beast and were making our way down the throat. Soon we'd be in the belly, where things would be sure to start happening. It'd be a gas. . .'

At the end of the hallway was a staircase that reached up to the ground floor of the building. As the A-Team moved stealthily up the steps, they could begin to hear voices. They proceeded cautiously, then remained hidden at the top of the stairs, which led to a large indoor garden room. An overhead skylight let the afternoon sun pour down on a selection of suspended planters and potted trees. A bar filled one wall, done up in a bamboo motif and well-stocked with a variety of liqueurs. Large silk-screens accented the other walls, depicting emperors and great warriors of ancient China, the type of men the Lung Chin, in their own twisted way, felt they emulated with their ruthless pursuit of power and possession. A glass archway opened out to a central courtyard, where several dozen young, black-garbed men were going through a series of martial arts manoeuvres. Inside the garden room, however, were men long past the age of karate kicks and ju-jitsu demonstrations. Wan Chu, the elder leader of the Lung Chin, sat at the head of a long table, his frail hands clasped before him. Sitting with him were other greyhaired men making up his general council. At his right side, too, was one exception to the geriatic make-up of the gathering. The broad-shouldered giant who had confronted the A-Team outside the headquarters earlier was listening to Wan Chu with full concentration.

'I want to talk to the people we are sending out tonight,' Wan Chu asked. 'Arrange it, Stan Ling.'

'They are out in the courtyard with the others,' the giant responded. 'They will be here for instructions in twenty minutes, Wan Chu.'

The old man nodded. 'That is good. If this plan succeeds, the futures of your sons will be secured.'

Stan Ling smiled thinly. 'They long to serve the Lung Chin as I have.'

Wan Chu looked out at his fellow elders. The light from overhead fell on his face and gave his features a radiance that suited his joyful anticipation. 'Just as our ancestors extended their empires through shrewd dealings and great conquests, so shall the Lung Chin expand its power in this land. We will move beyond the confines of –'

The chieftain was interrupted in mid-sentence by the sudden appearance of the A-Team, who had donned their masks as they charged into the room, guns blazing over the heads of those at the table.

'On your feet!' Hannibal barked at the council members. 'Hands in the air! All of you!'

The men at the table slowly rose, confused by the presence of the gunmen.

'What is this outrage?' Stan Ling shouted at the A-Team. 'This traitorous act must stop at once.'

'Sorry, but we're not traitors,' Hannibal said as he pulled off his mask. His associates did the same, and Ling's face went dark with recognition.'

'How did you get in here?' he demanded.

Peck replaced the clip on his rifle and grinned at the giant. 'I know a guy who had some tickets he wasn't using.'

Wan Chu stopped short of raising his hands over his head. He squinted at Hannibal and spoke with a voice that reeked of venom. 'You have violated the stronghold of the Lung Chin!'

'Yeah, it was really tough with that garage door opening up for us,' Hannibal said, swinging the gun in the direction of the aged leader. 'Now let's chop the mystical stronghold garbage and come up with the money-box pal.'

B.A. cocked his shotgun and drew aim on Wan Chu as well. 'Now!'

'Money-box?' Wan Chu frowned. 'For what? Who are

you?'

'We're part owners of the Golden Pagoda restaurant,' Hannibal said. 'We're here to get what's owed us because of what your apes did to it. By the way, those apes are cooling their heels outside your import shop on Tenth Street, in case no one's found them yet.'

'Like we told them,' Peck said, 'by our calculations you owe us fifty grand and a promise to stay away from our place in the future. An apology would be nice, but it's optional.'

'And we don't take credit cards,' Murdock pitched in 'Cold cash, tootsie, and you better make it quick, 'cause my finger's got an itch and my gun's got an urge to bark at somebody. When it comes to my gun, the bark's nothin' compared to the bite, either. . .'

'I know you,' Wan Chu said, squinting harder at Murdock. 'You have been in the motion pictures, no?'

'Just call him Bogie,' Hannibal said, stepping forward. 'But I'd suggest you quite stalling, because it only makes me mad, and when I get mad, I'm a regular bull in a china shop.'

By way of demonstration, Hannibal shot up the bar. Bamboo splintered from the impact of bullets and the glass shattered loudly, sounding like chimes on drugs. B.A. butchered a few bushes with shotgun blasts and Peck fired up at the skylight, bringing down a shower of glass shards that forced the council members to cover their heads in fear.

'Stop!' Wan Chu shouted.

'Hey, we're just warming up, ace!' Hannibal said.

Wan Chu turned to Stan Ling and nodded angrily. The giant moved away from the table and headed for the far wall. As he pulled aside one of the silkscreens and started fumbling with the dials of a wall safe, Murdock went over to keep an eye on him.

'Hear my gun whimpering, friend?' Murdock provided his own sound effects for the weapon, making Ling event more nervous. 'Boy, it wants to bark so bad I can taste it.'

As Ling opened the safe, the doors to the courtyard

opened and a handful of armed men poured into the room. Seeing that their leaders were under the gun, they did not fire their weapons. They looked to Wan Chu for a signal.

Hannibal advised, 'Better tell your boys to forget the heroics, Three Four.'

'My name is Wan Chu!'

'Wan Chu, three four, I keep losing count,' Hannibal wisecracked. 'Now tell you grandkids to line up against that wall behind you and put their noses against the wallpaper. Don't make me have to wipe out your whole generation, pops.'

Wan Chu addressed the soldiers in their native tongue and the young men sullenly moved over to the wall and turned their backs to the A-Team. B.A. and Peck went over to take their weapons from them. On the other side of the room, Stan Ling removed an ornately designed box that rested on a polished brass tray. Under Murdock's guard, he carried it over to the long table and set it before Wan Chu. The Chinese elder laid his withered fingers on the box, pressing some of the carved fixtures on it in a specific sequence until an inner lock clicked and allowed him to raise the lid. Inside the box was a roll of hundred dollar bills as thick as B.A.'s wrist. Wan Chu reached for it, but Hannibal beat him to it and handed the wad to Peck.

'Looks like there might be enough left over after you pay us to buy yourselves dinner,' Hannibal said.

'Gloat while you may,' Wan Chu said icily.

'Don't mind if I do,' Hannibal replied. Raising his voice for all the elders to hear, he went on, 'Now here's the new law. We're closing you down. And you don't have any choice. We can vanish. . . we can reappear at any time, kinda like fleas, only a lot more obnoxious. If we catch wind that the Lung Chin's trying to flex its muscle around town again, we'll be on you so fast you won't know what hit you.'

'I'll give you a hint, though,' B.A. flashed his fist a few inches in front of Wan Chu's face. 'It's gonna look something like this, only more blurry.'

'On whose authority do you make these threats?' Wan Chu wanted to know.

Hannibal patted the stock of his rifle. 'Here's all the authority I need. Now, we want you and your whole pond of Peking ducks to be outta this neighbourhood and outta people's lives by tomorrow. . . at two o'clock.'

'You are very funny,' Wan Chu said, closing the lid on the box.

'Coming from you, that means a lot,' Hannibal cracked. 'Tell you what, how about if we make it five after two. I mean, we're not unreasonable. That'll give you time to pack your thumb-screws.'

Peck finished peeling off fifty thousand dollars, then tossed the rest of the money onto the bronze tray. 'There should be enough there for you to hire out a junk for your junk. Thanks for the settlement. It's nice dealing with professionals.'

The A-Team backtracked to the stairway, keeping their guns aimed at the Lung Chin. Hannibal fired up a cigar, then told the Chinese gangsters, 'Remember, you can close yourselves down or we can close you down. Why not go the easy way? You know what doctors say about stress being such a killer.'

In unison, the A-Team started barrelling down the staircase, clearing two and three steps at a time. By the time they had reached the underground hallway, they could already hear the sounds of pursuit coming from behind them.

'You sure know how to stir up a hornets' nest, Hannibal,' Peck puffed as they ran down the hall. 'If those had been real daggers in Wan Chu's eyes, you'd be looking like a voodoo doll about now.'

'I wanted to speak in a language he understood,' Hannibal defended himself. 'He didn't look like the type that's very responsive to "pretty please".'

Back in the garage, five Lung Chin heavies had discovered the man B.A. had borrowed his outfit from, and when they saw the A-Team burst into view, they reached for their guns. Peck fired a round at their feet and shouted, 'Touch those guns and the next round goes a few feet higher.'

The gangsters froze in place and watched as the A-Team filed quickly into the same sedan they'd arrived in. As B.A. turned the ignition and revved up the engine, Murdock saw the young men from upstairs surging down the hallway toward the garage. 'The hotheads weren't taking "get lost" for an answer and they were getting real itchy to burn out our bulbs. We had only one choice, and we went for it. We made a break for it. Hurry up, B.A., let's make a break for it!'

As he shifted the sedan into reverse, B.A. looked over his shoulder and swore, 'Damn, the garage door ain't open!'

'One more time,' Murdock howled, ducking the first volley of gunfire that came whistling at the sedan. 'We make a *break* for it!'

B.A. gassed the engine and the sedan screeched backwards out of its parking space, bowling over two Lung Chin members before crashing through the garage door with the grinding din of metal clashing with metal. Carried by its own momentum, the sedan shot up the incline of the driveway and out into the street, almost colliding with traffic. A panel truck was forced to swerve sharply to one side, sending a pair of armed gunmen diving for cover before they had a chance to get off any shots at the A-Team. There were other Lung Chin crackshots roaming the street, however, and as the general alarm spread, B.A. found himself driving through a gauntlet of gunfire and other vehicles that tried crashing into the sedan with the reckless determination of kamikaze planes going after an aircraft carrier. The car took a few jolts and more than a few bullets, but kept rolling.

'Man, I'm sure glad this ain't my van gettin' chewed up like this!' B.A. said, jerking the steering wheel back and forth as he sped past the dwindling obstacles in his way. Without taking his eyes off the way before him, he called out, 'Everybody else okay?'

'Oh, fine, just fine,' Peck said, untangling himself in the back seat. 'This kinda reminds me of bus rides to junior high.' A bullet crashed through the window and buried itself in the armrest beside him. 'The spitballs are a little more heavyduty, though, I gotta admit.'

Murdock was hunched down next to Peck, his eyes darting wildly. 'Outside the car it sounded like New Years Eve,' he said, 'I was beginning to wonder if I was ever going to see the Maltese Cow now that we were fleeing its obvious pasture.

Hannibal turned around in the front seat and told Murdock, 'Don't worry, Hump, I got a feeling we're going to be seeing a lot more of the Lung Chin before this is over. . .'

TWENTY-THREE

Far to the north of Los Angeles, between the San Fernando Valley and the Mojave Desert, was Antelope Valley, a relatively barren stretch of land inhabited by a sparse population that, for the most part, lived in scattered colonies of tract homes. Just outside such a tract in the small town of Del Sur, friends of Tommy Chen owned a horse ranch on more than two hundred acres of land. Far back in the rear corner of the property was a small guest cabin, surrounded by a thin belt of Joshua pines and backed by a jagged escarpment of basalt. It was to the cabin that Tommy Chen took his parents to hide. They had stocked up a week's worth of groceries, and Tommy had made certain that his father knew how to use the Model 71 Winchester hunting rifle that his friend kept in the cabin. Against Hannibal's advice, the younger Chen had decided not to join his parents in their seclusion. Once he had seen to it that they were settled in, he got back into the family station wagon and headed back for Los Angeles. He was going to stay with the Lung Chin, but only so he could monitor their movements and try to think of a way he could help see to their undoing.

The sun had been down for more than an hour when Chen returned to Chinatown. Dressed in the garb of the Lung Chin, he gained admittance to the headquarters without contest, although he was berated slightly for arriving several minutes later than the time he had been told to arrive for a meeting called by Wan Chu himself. When he slipped into the large assembly hall where the elder chieftain was addressing two dozen of his men, Chen felt everyone's eyes turn on him and his face turned red with supposed embarrassment. Stan Ling and Wan Chu both eyed Chen severely, but neither so much as spoke to him. Wan Chu paced in slow, measured steps before his assembled force, mulling over his words before he spoke them.

'We have two objectives tonight,' he finally began. 'Number one is to insure the safe arrival of Mr Thomas into this country. You have all been instructed in this task, and it will proceed smoothly.'

As Wan Chu spoke, he gazed at the young men before him, searching their faces for any sign of doubt or frailty that might undermine their efficiency as agents of his will. The majority of men stared ahead with the firm, locked stare of obedient attention that he sought. Several however, either met the elder's gaze or deliberately looked away from him, and he was equally suspicious of both reactions. When he was in front of Tommy Chen, Wan Chu watched the new recruit for several eternal seconds. Chen concentrated every ounce of his will power into staring straight ahead and betraying no sign of weakness. His was a convincing exhibition, because Wan Chu finally walked on and began testing another of the soldiers.

'Objective number two,' he went on, 'is revenge for the insult brought upon the Lung Chin today.'

The mere word 'revenge' ran like ice down Chen's spine when Wan Chu spoke it. He made it sound as if there were no greater satisfaction in the world than the extraction of revenge, just as there was no bleaker fate to befall anyone who became the target of Wan Chu's wrath.

'The Golden Pagoda restaurant must be destroyed as well as the people who own it!' Wan Chu fervently declared. 'If such a threat to us goes unanswered, Mr Thomas will not be inclined to let us handle most of his drug business in this city. I would not blame him if this were the case, for only a fool would deal with anyone who cannot rise above his enemies.' The old man paused to make certain that his words sank in, then concluded, 'You have your work. Now go, and when you return, it will be with the results I desire, or you will not return at all.'

Wan Chu turned abruptly and left the room. Stan Ling remained behind, staring at his charges. 'Anyone who fails in this mission will answer to me!' he vowed, then clapped his hands.

With the precision of a finely-tooled machine, the Lung Chin marched from the assembly room and down the hall to the three trucks that would take them to the docks in San Pedro. Tommy Chen knew that he had only a few minutes to do what he planned. He slipped away from the others and ducked down a side hallway to a pay phone mounted on the wall. After looking around to make certain he was alone, he put a dime into the phone and carefully dialled the number jotted down on a scrap of paper he removed from his shirt pocket. He waited impatiently for an answer on the other line and was finally rewarded on the seventh ring by the sound of his beloved's voice.

'Hello?'

'Sun, this is Tommy,' Chen whispered hurriedly. 'I can't say much but I had to call. There are orders –'

A hand suddenly reached out and clamped itself over Chen's mouth. Another hand took the receiver from him and hung it up, then spun Chen around, much the way Hannibal had done to get his attention at the laundry. Chen found himself staring up at Stan Ling, who was smiling savagely.

'You have done well, Tommy Chen. You have led us to where Sam and Sun Yeng are hiding.'

'No!' Chen gasped frantically, trying to break the giant's ironclad grip on him.

Stan Ling pried open Chen's fingers and removed the slip of paper with the telephone number on it. 'Yes,' he murmured. 'Yes!'

Chen saw that it was futile to argue further. He had

been caught, and caught red-handed. His heart began to pound hard against his ribcage and fear ran through his system like a strong poison, making him shake.

'We knew that if we gave you enough room, you would lead us to them,' Ling taunted. 'I think it is safe for us to assume as well that you have warned the white men about tonight's plans. That is just as well, for it will not make it necessary for us to look for them. We shall, as the Americans say, kill two birds with one stone. . .'

TWENTY-FOUR

The docks were like something straight out of a hard-boiled novel, rundown and weary, shrouded in a veil of evening fog. Idle cranes and machinery stood about like dinosaurs frozen in a trance of lethargy. There were boats out in the harbour, mostly large freighters with swollen holds, bound for port in the great name of international commerce. Their horns bellowed lowly through the night, scattering the gulls that hovered above the leaping waves. At Pier 52, the A-Team was couched behind a stack of weathered crates, armed with AR-15s as they peered out at the cargo ship moored nearby. The Lung Chin were patrolling the area around the boarding ramp, looking like unembodied shadows in their black regalia. Two familiar-looking sedans were parked nearby, gleaming under the lamplight that fell on their fog-beaded exteriors. Hannibal was looking through a pair of binoculars at the main deck of the vessel. Beside him, Murdock was basking in the atmosphere.

'The fog was thicker than a linebacker's neck and the sun was blocked from view like a stranger with bad breath,' he said. 'Anything could happen on a day like this, or maybe nothing. All I could do was wait and try to keep my nerves from turning to knots I'd never be able to untie.'

B.A. nudged Peck. 'Tell that fool it's night, not day here!'

148

'Murdock, it's night,' Peck said. 'Make a note of it, okay?'

Murdock thought it over, then amended his soliloquy. 'The fog was thicker than the accent of a bad Russian actor doing Shakespeare and the moon was like the glaring monocle of a one-eyed critic condemning the performance.' He looked over his shoulder at B.A. and asked, 'How's that?'

'I oughta pack you in one of these crates and get you shipped to some island where nobody'd have to put up with your jive, fool!'

Peck smirked, 'Gee, Murdock, I was sure I was going to hear something about the foghorns sounding like the lament of the Maltese Cow.'

'Too obvious,' Murdock said.

Hannibal lowered his binoculars. 'Well, the gang's all there. We're pretty well outnumbered, so I think we should start out with a good diversion. Face? Feel like pulling out a few rabbits?'

'Do I have a choice?'

'Not really.'

'That's what I thought.' Peck surveyed the area around the boarding ramp, considering his possibilities. 'Give me ten minutes,' he finally said as he broke away from the others and vanished into the shadows. He made his way down the narrow passageway between old wharves to where the van was parked. Slipping inside, he quickly changed out of his black garb and into a stylish Ralph Lauren ensemble. He borrowed a false moustache and some tinted glasses from Hannibal's make-up kit, then grabbed a few stray sheets of paper and emerged from the van looking like a refugee from the pages of Gentleman's Quarterly. Whistling nonchalantly, he strode down the pier in the direction of the Lung Chin heavies guarding the boarding ramp.

'Excuse me, guys,' he told them, 'I hate to bother you, but I'm looking for the Felicity Cruises tour ship.'

The two guards before him glanced at one another, then one of them said, 'Not here.'

Peck unfolded the papers in his hand and ran his finger along the prose. 'My tour director is. . . yes, here it is. . . Bud Pillsbury?'

'Get lost,' the second guard said, shifting his rifle in his hands for emphasis.

Behind the guards, Peck could see Hannibal, B.A., and Murdock moving away from the crates and inching toward the ship by way of whatever other cover there was for them to hide behind. 'Say,' Peck addressed the Lung Chin, keeping up the diversion, 'you guys. . . you don't work here, do you?'

'This is a cargo ship,' the first guard snapped. 'We work security. There aren't any tour ships at this pier. Ain't no Bud Pillsbury, either.'

'A cargo ship, you say. . .' Peck let his gaze stroll up the boarding ramp to the main deck. 'Boy, it sure looks to me like you could play shuffleboard up there.' He referred back to his would-be tourist papers. 'So you're sure you don't have something called the *Cinco De Mayo* deck on this ship? With a donkey ride? Complimentary piñata?'

'You got the wrong end of the harbour,' the first guard said, lowering his rifle and pointing it at Peck. 'I ain't gonna tell you again.'

Hannibal and B.A. were now as close as the parked sedans. Peck took a deep breath, filled with frustration. 'This is a real letdown, I'm telling ya! I mean, I was supposed to have this great cabin on the Pancho Villa Promenade. What a bummer. I've tried to take a cruise for over six years. Six years, can you believe it? It's for my sinuses, you see. They're clogged up all the time. Just listen to me. . .' He inhaled through his nose, making a sound like a malfunctioning fog-horn. 'And this is a good day.'

Both guards were about to physically escort Peck away from the ramp when they were suddenly grabbed from behind by B.A. and Hannibal. Before the Lung Chin could mouth a warning to their confederates, Murdock bopped each of them on the back of the head with the butt of his rifle, sending them on a personalized cruise to the world of their dreams.

'At least it's a good day for some of us,' Peck told the slumping gangsters. 'Hannibal, I'm glad you guys finally made it. They were about ready to book me for a ride on the ship's propeller.'

As B.A. and Murdock were dragging the unconscious men off behind one of the sedans, three more Lung Chin suddenly appeared out of the blackness, hurtling toward the A-Team like exhibitionists trying out for a musical based on the life of Bruce Lee. Hannibal ducked under the flailing limbs of his opponent, then swung his rifle like a home run hitter reaching for an outside curveball. The gun's barrel knocked the wind out of the black-clad warrior, and while he was gasping for breath, Hannibal gave him a karate chop that sent him sprawling to the planks. Peck snatched up one of the fallen guard's rifles and held it in front of him to ward off a deadly kick by another foe. The rifle cracked in half as if it were no more than a dried twig. Peck let go of it and, in the same motion, grabbed his attacker's ankle and raised it as high as he could. Losing his balance, the Lung Chin warrior fell backwards, slamming his head against the pier. That left one attacker, who closed in on Murdock. Murdock rose like a matador without a cape and deftly sidestepped the advancing gangster. Before the man could turn around for a second charge, B.A. moved in and polished him off with a series of rabbit punches. Murdock came over to help B.A. ease the victim down to the planks.

'I owe you one, big guy.'

'Good,' B.A. said. 'Then shut up!'

Hannibal aimed his AR-15 at the main deck of the cargo ship in case anyone there had heard the scuffling, but no one appeared. The others dragged the downed Lung Chin out of sight and tied them up, then rejoined Hannibal near the boarding ramp.

'What now?' Peck asked.

Hannibal waved in the direction of the ramp. 'All aboard. . .'

TWENTY-FIVE

Chris Thomas was a tall, thick-chested man with a receding hairline and incredibly thick eyebrows that dominated his olive-skinned features, lurking over his cold grey eyes like a mutant strain of caterpillars, crouched and ready to leap out at anyone who came too close to him. He wore a dark homburg and knee-length fogcoat and carried himself with the self-assured air of an ambassador who knew his every action was protected by the blanket of diplomatic immunity. Part of his confidence came from within; the rest was provided by his coterie of bodyguards, three strapping bulks who looked like disgruntled runners-up in the Mr Olympia competition who had just found out that the winner was a feminist transsexual. Of course, Thomas was anything but a diplomat. Crime was his element, and in the presence of Stan Ling and a handful of Lung Chin warriors, he felt among his own kind. As such, he didn't trust Ling for a second.

'There better not be any cops out there,' Thomas said as he paced the stateroom of the cargo ship, occasionally veering to one of the portholes and peering out into the fog-choked night. ''Cause if there are, I can still claim asylum just by staying right where I am. You know, my Libyan registry still covers me while I'm on the ship.'

'The Lung Chin will take you safely into the city,' Ling confided to the crime figure. 'We will reach our head-

152

quarters without incident, you can be sure of it.'

'We'd better.' Thomas went over to the table in the middle of the room and picked up a bundle the size of a football, wrapped with a coarse dark cloth and bound with heavy twine. 'Let's go.'

Stan Ling stepped forward and reached for the object Thomas had tucked under his arm. 'May we carry that for you?'

'I don't even want you to touch it,' Thomas responded coldly as he tightened his grip on the bundle the way a linebacker grips the ball before forging ahead with an end sweep. 'Is that clear?'

Ling was a head taller than Thomas, and he had to battle back an urge to put the other man in his place. However, he had his orders from Wan Chu, and knew that if he did anything to ruffle Thomas's feathers his standing with the Lung Chin would be gravely jeopardized. Ling nodded tersely to the man in the homburg, then turned and headed for the door. Before he could reach it, the door burst inward and Peck charged into the stateroom, peppering the ceiling with blasts from his AR-15. Murdock followed close behind, but levelled his gun at the men gathered around the table.

'Reach for it!' Peck demanded between blasts. 'Now!'

Startled by the sudden change of events, Thomas put his hands up and took a step backwards to get behind one of his bodyguards. His bundle fell from beneath his arm and hit the polished slats of the stateroom floor with a sickening thud. Whatever was inside the bundle broke and the man's face turned an anguished shade of ash.

'Okay, boys, just stay the way you are and nobody gets hurt.' Peck glanced down at the fallen bundle, then told Murdock, 'Let's see what the doorprize is tonight, shall we? I sure hope it isn't a blender, because I just got one for my birthday.'

'Who are you?' Thomas demanded.

'The welcome wagon, Mr Thomas,' Peck drawled. 'Sorry we couldn't bring cookies, but they got left in the oven too long. We brought some hot lead, though, and if

153

you want some, all you gotta do is ask for it.'

Nobody was willing to take on Peck's rifle. They stood, mute and angry, and watched as Murdock retrieved the bundle from the floor and set it on the table. He untied the knots and began to unravel the cloth wrapping.

'What's it going to be, Thomas?' Peck speculated. 'Uncut heroin? Opium? A kilo of cocaine?'

'I couldn't believe my eyes,' Murdock gasped as he uncovered a fragmented clay sculpture. It looked ancient and well-crafted, but it wasn't the provenance of the piece that left Murdock breathless so much as the shape. Although it seemed to have an extra horn, there was an unmistakable bovine appearance to the sculpture. 'After all these years, was it possible I'd finally laid eyes on the ever-elusive Maltese Cow?'

Murdock was so enthralled by his find that he dropped his guard, allowing Stan Ling to lash out with a karate kick that sent Murdock staggering backwards in the direction of his partner. Murdock had dropped his rifle and Peck wasn't able to use his with Murdock blocking the way, and all at once the stateroom was a fenzy of turmoil as Lung Chin and Thomas's bodyguards allied together in a charge on their mutual foes. When Hannibal and B.A. barged in moments later, they found Murdock and Peck sandwiched amidst the swarm of enemy limbs. Before Hannibal could fire a round of warning shots, two Lung Chin were on him. One wrested the rifle from Hannibal's hands and threw it to the ground while the other tried using Hannibal's head as a punching bag. B.A. was attacked from both sides, and while he was fending off the man on his right, Stan Ling moved up behind him and delivered a blow to the base of B.A.'s skull that took the fight out of him for the time being.

As the A-Team continued to wage its uphill battle in the cramped confines of the stateroom, Chris Thomas grabbed his bundle and cradled it in his arms as he slipped out onto the deck. Stan Ling ran alongside him as they hurried down the boarding ramp, searching the pier for signs of the authorities.

'What is that thing?' Lind asked, glancing at the ceramic figurine as he opened one of the sedan doors for Thomas.

'Junk,' Thomas confessed with a sardonic grin, 'but it makes a nice microfilm case.'

'Microfilm?' Ling said. 'Of what?'

'That's my concern, Mr Ling. Now let's get out of here, fast!' Thomas pointed across the harbour to a series of flashing lights. He could already hear the first wailing of sirens. 'I don't want to be around when the heat shows up.!'

As Ling and Thomas drove off, their underlings continued to do battle with the A-Team inside the stateroom. The Team was making a resurgence, insofar as they were all still conscious and two of their adversaries were out cold. The stateroom had taken a worse beating than either side, since anything that wasn't bolted down had been grabbed and used as a weapon. Brief duels had been fought with wastebaskets against hat racks, paperweights against shipping logs. Finally the fighting spilled out onto the deck, and the A-Team was beginning to get the upper hand. B.A. sent one of Thomas's bodyguards reeling over the side and into the cold waters of the harbour, then strode over to help Murdock fend off a pair of Lung Chin. Peck borrowed a few tricks from the 'Douglas Fairbanks Book of Heroics' and vaulted himself through the air, grabbing hold of a guy wire to enable him to swing his toe with enough force to knock out a thug who was reaching to his shoulder holster for a .44 Magnum. Hannibal broke a small crate over someone's head, then found himself grappling someone else who had grabbed him from behind.

All the while, the sound of the sirens drew closer and soon the flashing lights atop the roofs of a half-dozen squad cars were cutting through the fog at Pier 52. A SWAT truck brought up the rear, then braked to a halt and a dozen crack sharpshooters piled out to join the twenty-odd policemen who had left the squad cars to converge upon the moored cargo ship. In the midst of all this law enforcement was the man in charge, a rumpled, balding man with lambchop sideburns and drooping eyes. His name was Capers, and he was dressed in a grey suit. He stared up at the fighting on the docks, letting the A-Team dispatch a few more of the Lung Chin over the side of the ship before raising a bullhorn to his lips and shouting, 'Freeze!'

Almost forty guns and rifles backed up the order, and as soon as the men on the deck noticed them, the fighting was over.

TWENTY-SIX

'It was just a coincidence, Murdock.'

'No, Face, it was a cow.'

The A-Team was in police custody, being marched down the main corridor at the division station by a pair of uniformed officers. Capers was with them, too, burning his way through his third cigarette in the past ten minutes. He listened to Peck and Murdock arguing, wondering what kind of secret code they might be talking in.

'You're jumping to conclusions, Murdock,' Peck insisted. 'It could have been a dragon, or a water buffalo. . . maybe some kinda flying monster. You know, Son of Godzilla.'

'No, it had to be the Maltese Cow,' Murdock maintained. 'I'd bet my wife on it.'

'You don't have a wife, Murdock.'

Capers dropped his cigarette on the linoleum and crushed it out, then popped a fresh one in his mouth as he interjected, 'Okay, now we know the clown with the fedora is named Murdock. That's an encouraging sign, here. How about if the rest of you wise up and give me your names, too.'

'My mother always told me to keep my name,' Hannibal cracked as he and the others were ushered into the detective's office. 'I'll stick to mom's advice, thanks.'

Capers gestured for the prisoners to be seated as he circled around behind his cluttered desk. He opened the window behind his desk and dumped out what was left in the bottom of his personalized coffee mug, then filled the cup with a fresh batch from the coffee maker on the filing cabinet next to the desk. Slumping into his chair, he glanced warily at the A-Team, noting that Murdock was still talking in code.

'It was a cow, man,' Murdock told Face. 'Definite moo-moo. It was exactly like I saw it in my mind, I'm tellin' ya. There's no use tryin' to pretend otherwise. I mean, look, I know I have this. . . zesty fantasy life, okay? But I never had it come right outta the woodwork and give milk like that. It was scary. . . another hard dose of destiny!'

'Man, I wish they woulda put handcuffs on your mouth, sucker!' B.A. complained, crossing his legs in his chair. 'There's gotta be a law against babblin'!'

Capers addressed the two officers who had accompanied him into the room. 'Linglas, call Nichols in psych and tell him we got a guy seein' cows up here in Sanders's office. Washington, check in with Aldonton and see if he's pumped those other prisoners for any info yet. I'll see what I can get out of the comedy troupe here.' As the other two officers left the room, Capers waved smoke out of his face and told Hannibal, 'You guys aren't exactly throwing us for a loop, you know. We may not have your names yet, but we do have your prints. I'm sure the computers will put a finger on you soon enough, then we'll start going through the book to see how many charges we can throw against you.'

'Remember that old television commercial for some brand of aspirin?' Hannibal asked Capers. 'You know, the one where the poor chump with the migraine is making life miserable for everyone until his best buddy drags him aside and tells him, "Of course you have a headache, but you don't have to take it out on us." '

'What the hell does that have to do with anything?' Capers demanded, blowing over the brim of his cup before sipping the hot brew that was like fuel to him.

'I think you're putting us on the grill because one of your bosses is hot over you lettin' Chris Thomas slip through your fingers.' Hannibal saw Capers flinch at the accusation. 'Screwups like that can end up getting you transferred to juvenile duty, can't they? You're just sore because you don't like the prospects of chasing the hookie crowd outta the Seven-Elevens after school starts. Isn't that it?'

'I don't know what you're talking about, pal,' Capers said.

'We could deliver him to you,' Hannibal said. 'I'm talking about Thomas.'

Peck seconded, 'Yeah, we could nail that goon in no time. . . provided we didn't have a row of bars between us and doing it.

'This isn't *"Let's Make a Deal",*' Capers said. 'I don't need your help to do my job.'

'It's after eleven,' Peck lobbied, 'The rates are lower. Sure you won't reconsider?'

The squawkbox on the desk bleeped, then a thin, tinny voice crackled, 'Detective Capers? This is Casvensol in the computer room. There's nobody on duty down here who knows how to run a trace on those prints you wanted me to check out. Wirz is out on break for another twenty minutes. You want I should wait till he gets back?'

'No, I'll be down and run the check myself,' Capers barked into the intercom. He drained the last of his coffee, then moved out from behind the desk. 'I'll be right back, boys. If you're thinking of trying anything, remember that I'm still looking for something solid to arrest you on, and if you leave this room I'll have all I need to toss you behind bars. Understood?'

Hannibal leaned forward and flicked on the small portable television perched on the corner of the desktop 'Don't worry, they've got Jackie Gleason reruns on and we wouldn't dream of missing them. If you could bring back some popcorn, though, it'd be wonderful.'

'What I bring back isn't apt to be wonderful.'

Once Capers left the room and closed the door behind him, B.A. got up and went to the window. He opened it and stared out, then pulled his head back in and shook it.

159

'Three storeys straight down to a lot filled with cop cars. We ain't goin' that way!'

Hannibal turned the television back off and stared out the window, not focusing on anything in particular. Peck glanced at him. 'I hear clocks ticking, Hannibal. There's the our-fingerprints-are-gonna-give-us-away-clock, and the let's-take-Murdock-back-to-the-bozo-barn-clock.'

Murdock cupped a hand behind his ear and frowned. 'I don't hear a thing. Not even a moo.'

'We gotta do something, Hannibal,' B.A. said. 'Once he finds out who we are, he's gonna put us in chains until Colonel Decker can cruise by to toss us in the brig!'

'I think I'll reach out and touch someone,' Hannibal decided, grabbing the phone off the desk and punching for the dispatcher. 'Locker room, please.'

'What are you doing, Hannibal?' Peck whispered.

Hannibal held up a hand for the others to be silent, then cleared his throat and growled into the receiver, 'Yeah, this is Detective Sanders. Listen, I spilled some coffee and a bearclaw on my uniform and I can't get down there to grab my other ones. . . Yeah, yeah, it's nutzo up here. Everybody's going up in flames 'cause Capers blew the Thomas bust down at the docks. . . You got it. Anyway, Captain's comin' in and I don't want to look like I got the shakes or something. So do you have somebody down there who can run that extra uniform up to me. . . Yeah? Hey, that's dynamite, man! You're a pal. I'd buy you coffee sometime but I'd probably get it all over you. . . Right, 'bye.' Hannibal hung up and grinned at his fellow prisoners. 'Everybody loves a good story, right, guys?'

'I don't believe you, Hannibal,' Peck said. 'I mean, you were lucky enough to fool the dim bulb down in the locker room that you were this Detective Sanders, but I've got twenty bucks that says the flunky who tries toting that spare uniform up here won't make it past the first floor before they figure out something's not right.'

'You're on.'

Less than five minutes later, the door to the office opened and a young cop strode in, carrying the requested uniform. Peck groaned and reached for his moneyclip as the officer asked, 'Where's Sanders?'

'Don't ask me,' Hannibal sneered, changing his voice dramatically from the one he's used on the phone. 'We're here to be booked, right? I guess he's comin' back 'cause he's supposed to book us. . . right? I mean, we are bein' booked, aren't we? We ain't here to donate blood, that's for sure!'

'Spare me the lip,' the officer said, draping the uniform over the back of one of the chairs. 'Tell him this is his. He asked for it. You think you can remember that?'

'Can ducks play the blues?' Hannibal asked cryptically.

The officer made a disgusted face on his way out of the room. Peck seemed equally upset as he handed Hannibal a ten dollar bill and two ones. 'I owe you the rest.'

'You've got a lousy credit rating, Face,' Hannibal said as he got up from his seat. 'You're going to have to cough up some collateral to go with this.'

Peck tossed Hannibal the empty moneyclip, which had his birthstone mounted on its facing. 'There.'

Hannibal slipped the clip into the shirt pocket of the uniform, which he quickly changed into while Murdock stood near the door and peered out to make sure Capers wasn't returning yet. Apparently Detective Sanders was one of the bigger men on the force, because his uniform was large on Hannibal.

'I guess I can say I just raided a spa, huh?' he cracked. 'Okay, let's see how far we can get. Face, you want to go double or nothing? I say we'll be outta here in three minutes.'

'Forget it,' Peck said. 'I'm through betting against us.'

Hannibal opened the door and ushered his confederates out into the hallway. He saw the exit sign posted at the end of the corridor and started leading the others to it. They passed by several offices with their doors closed, then Hannibal gestured for everyone to freeze. They were outside the Captain's office, and Capers could be heard talking to another man, presumably the Captain himself.

'I just ran through a computer request on their prints,'

Capers was saying. 'Results should be back any second. I got a feeling they might be part of England Dave's gang. They've been spatting on and off with the Lung Chin more than anybody else besides us.'

'Okay,' the other man said, 'Take 'em to interrogation and see if you can get something out of them one way or another, even if they don't ID as part of England's gang.'

'Will do, Captain.'

Hannibal motioned for Peck, B.A., and Murdock to hurry past him to the stairwell, then he made a break for it himself, managing to slip through the door just as Capers was leaving the Captain's office.

'Whew!' Murdock muttered. 'I could go to the best barber in town and not be able to get a closer shave.'

The A-Team started down the staircase. When a pair of officers entered the stairwell from the second floor and started up the steps, Hannibal stiffened and commanded his partners, 'All right, move it, you guys! Quit yer stallin'!'

Fortunately, the two other officers were engrossed in their own conversation and didn't give Hannibal more than a cursory glance. He exhaled and led his men down to the ground floor. The A-Team still had more than a minute and a half to make good on Hannibal's prognosis for their escape, and it was beginning to look as if he'd overestimated the difficulty they would encounter. But then a boyish-looking officer suddenly burst into the stairwell, clutching a ripped sheet from a teletype machine. His eyes were alive with the kind of excitement children have when they possess news that no one else has heard yet. Because he was re-reading the message on the paper, he almost collided with Hannibal.

'What's your hurry, officer?' Hannibal snapped, bringing the man to a quick state of attention. 'You look like you just got your first kiss.'

'I'm sorry, sir,' the young man siad, his eyes still gleaming. 'It's just that they don't know who they have upstairs.'

'And who's that?' Hannibal said, moving so that he

162

took up most of the officer's field of vision. Behind him, the others tried their best to look like run-of-the-mill convicts rather than men who had been the focus of the Army's longest ongoing manhunt since the war in Indochina had been turned over to its own people.

'The A-Team!' the officer enthused, flashing the teletype page under Hannibal's face. There were no pictures on the readout, and the message stated that full physical descriptions were to follow shortly.

'The what team?' Hannibal asked.

'The A-Team! You know, those mercenaries you're always hearing about on those news shows. I mean, those guys are hot!' The young man snickered with ecstasy. 'And nobody upstairs knows it yet! Oh, man are they gonna flip over this one!'

'I'm sure you're right,' Hannibal said, stepping aside to let the officer bound merrily upstairs.

'Man, that dude's the one who's gonna flip when they find out he let us slip past him,' B.A. said.

'We're not out of here yet,' Hannibal reminded him as he opened the door to the main floor hallway. He pointed across the hall to an alcove filled with vending machines. 'Now, why don't you guys wait for me there while I try to track down some car keys. If anyone comes by, make sure you've got your hands behind your back like you're handcuffed. If they ask you anything, pretend you don't speak English.'

'Aw, great!' Murdock bubbled. 'Can we pretend to be Austrian? Huh? Huh?'

'You can pretend you got a broken mouth or I'll give you the real thing!' B.A. taunted as he and Murdock followed Peck to the alcove.

Hannibal ventured down the hallway, making himself as inconspicuous as possible. He'd lost track of the time, but he was beginning to feel glad he hadn't bet Peck on a getaway time. He didn't see any way to get his hands on a set of car keys without drawing too much attention his way. He was about to decide that they were going to have to make their break on foot when a pair of patrol officers suddenly entered the building, struggling to keep a defiant prostitute from wrenching free of their grip on her.

'Hey, give us a hand!' one of the men shouted at Hannibal. When he moved over to join them, he was told, 'Grab my cuffs and slap them on her before she gets her hands free. She's got fingernails like tiger claws!' The man who was speaking had long cuts down his cheek to prove it.

'Stinkin' pigs, get your hands off me!' the prostitute shrieked, fighting even harder now that the odds had increased even more against her. Hannibal kept bumping up against the other two officers as he carried out his orders and managed to get the woman into the handcuffs.

'Thanks,' the ranking officer told Hannibal. 'Say, I don't recognize you. . .'

'Detective Hannibal from Ramparts,' Hannibal bluffed. 'Down here on temporary transfer. Some of our locals apparently have their fingers in some smuggling operations at the harbour.'

'Well, good luck on that, and thanks again for this.'

'Any time.' Hannibal nodded to the men, then headed back down the hallway with a new acquisition jangling in his closed hand. He found the rest of the Team where he'd left them.

'I don't want to ever hear anything about me doin' bizarro things again, Hannibal,' Murdock said. 'Man, leavin' us like sittin' ducks like that was crazy! I mean, I didn't even have any change for the vending machines! You know how hard it is to *pretend* you're buyin' a pack of gum?'

'It's that jazz,' B.A. said, noting the spark in Hannibal's eye. 'Hannibal got himself juiced on the jazz. . .'

'Well, at this stage I'm ready for easy-listening, know what I mean?' Peck said. 'Hannibal, did you have any luck?'

Hannibal dangled the set of keys he'd picked from the pocket of one of the officers. 'Gentlemen, let's start our engines. . .'

Outside the station, there were seven patrol cars parked along the front curb near the entrance where the officers had come in with the prostitute. Hannibal checked the key ring to see if it might have a clue as to which of the cars it belonged to, but all the vehicles were of the same make.

'We don't have time to try each one,' he mused. Upstairs, he could already hear shouting in the vicinity of the office they'd escaped from.

'Check the hoods and see which ones are warm!' Peck suddenly blurted out, rushing down to the farthest car. The others split up and inspected the other vehicles. Only three of the cars had been driven recently, and Hannibal tried fitting the key into the ignition of the one with the warmest hood. It was a good guess, as the car started up immediately. The others quickly joined him, and the car shot out into the street, rooflights flashing to aid in the escape.

'Sam and Sun have the van at the hotel we sent 'em to,' Hannibal said as he drove, 'so we'll go there first. Then we'll have our firepower and we can pay a final visit to the Lung Chin and feed 'em their chopsticks.'

TWENTY-SEVEN

Traffic was light this late at night, and the A-Team made good time travelling north on the Long Beach Freeway. Along the stretch of roadway between San Pedro and the Olympic Boulevard turnoff in East Los Angeles, they passed almost two dozen other patrol cars, most of them belonging to the Highway Patrol. In each instance, B.A. would don the extra police cap that had been left in the car so that he would look like Hannibal's partner, while Murdock and Peck would play the role of apprehended felons. During the various conversations Hannibal had over the car radio, he embellished the alleged crimes of his would-be captives. Murdock and Peck had started out being petty car thieves, but by the end they had gained notoriety as being two of Crazy Tommy Tillis's hired guns that had somehow managed to escape capture during the grand melee at Mickey Stern's construction site on Federal and Denomville.

Once they left the freeway, the A-Team proceeded east on Olympic, passing through Commerce and into Montebello. A few blocks shy of the Rio Hondo waterway, Hannibal turned up a side street and proceeded to a small, out-of-the-way motel tucked back in the far corner of a weed-stewn lot. The motel was one of those establishments that charged hourly rates to anyone who knew enough to slip the clerk a hefty tip. What used to be lawn area around the main building had been paved over with asphalt, and even the drooping palm tree near the main entrance was maintenance-free plastic. The vacancy sign was blinking erratically, providing creative challenges for the flying insects that repeatedly bombarded it. A dozen cars were parked in a protective cluster under the lone streetlight, like a herd guarding itself against attack by carnivores. One vehicle, however, stood off to one side, half-hidden in shadow, and when B.A. spotted it he thumped his fist angrily on the dashboard of the patrol car.

'Hey, there's something wrong with my van!'

'How can you tell?' Peck said, peering out the window into the darkness. 'I can hardly see a thing.'

'Let's check this out,' Hannibal said as he drove past the other parked cars and flashed the patrol car headlights on the van, revealing that it was tilting heavily to one side.

'B.A., I have to say you have an extraordinary relationship with that van of yours,' Peck said. 'I mean, knowing there's something wrong just by driving into the parking lot, why, it's mind-boggling, it really –'

'All you gotta do is look, man!' B.A. scowled. 'Both tyres on the driver's side are flat, and I got a feeling it wasn't an accident. Damn!'

Hannibal parked near the van and everyone got out to inspect the damage. Murdock lingered behind to offer a commentary on what the others had found. 'I'd been a snoop-for-lease a lot of laps around the calendar, and I had some interesting advice for any interested schnook – a blowout and a tyre that was shot out were as different as rolling your own and buying 'em out of a machine. And it didn't matter if it was an 85 machine, or a 90 machine, or even a dollar a pack ma –'

'Shut up!' Peck, B.A., and Hannibal all hissed at Murdock simultaneously.

'Something told me to shut up,' Murdock mumbled under his breath as he stepped back from the others. 'Call it instinct. . .'

To the men's surprise, the inside of the van hadn't been vandalized. A few random items had been taken, but the footlockers hadn't been tampered with. As Hannibal unlocked the one with their spare weapons, he said, 'I think whoever broke in here must have left in a hurry because somebody was coming or something. They tripped the outside locks with no problems, so it had to be pros. They wouldn't have gone without at least having a look at these unless they didn't have a choice.'

'I just hope that whoever broke in here didn't do the same to the room where Sam and Sun are staying,' Peck said, loading the pistol Hannibal handed him.

'There's only one way we're going to find out,' Hannibal said. Once all four of them were armed, they left the van and circled around to the outside staircase leading up to the second storey of the motel. Lights were on in the room they were headed for, and they slowed down as they approached it. After crawling under the lit window, the foursome poised outside the door. Hannibal raised the fingers of one hand for a silent countdown. On zero, B.A. kicked the door open and Hannibal charged past him into the room, his gun pointed out in front of him as he shouted, 'Sam and Sun, duck!'

But Sam and Sun weren't there to duck. The apartment was empty, but it had been ripped apart from carpet to ceiling. The main room was a complete shambles, and the bathroom and kitchen areas weren't much better off. The walls were covered with Chinese characters written with red paint, the colour of blood.

'How'd they find out the Yengs were here?' Hannibal muttered, going up to one of the walls and running his finger across the red lettering. Wet paint came off on his fingertip. 'Couldn't have happened too long ago. I wonder what this says?'

' "Death to enemies of the Lung Chin",' Murdock said as he emerged from the bathroom.

'Come off it, Murdock,' Peck said. 'You aren't trying to tell us you can understand Chinese.'

Murdock shrugged his shoulders. 'What can I say? One day I had this gonzo headache, and by the time it went away, I was well-versed in Chinese and Serbo-Croat.

Weird, huh?'

B.A. stuck his head in the bathroom, then strode over and grabbed Murdock by the collar. 'Hey, turkey, you just read what one of them scrawled on the bathroom mirror with lipstick!'

Hannibal sorted through some of the mess, picking up an emptied suitcase belonging to Sun Yeng. He sat down on the edge of the ravaged bed and let his mind go to work on piecing together a plan of attack.

'Where do you think they took them?' Peck wondered aloud. 'Back to the Lung Chin headquarters?'

Hannibal nodded. 'I think so. I also bet that's where our buddy Thomas is headed, if he isn't there already. Matter of fact, I think the whole gang's probably there by now.'

'Great!' Peck said. 'Then all we have to do is make an anonymous phone call to the police and let them step in and do the dirty work.'

'Face, I'm disappointed in you,' Hannibal said. 'You really don't think we could even *consider* letting the police do our work for us, do you?'

'Why not?' Peck argued. 'Look, we've played hero more than our share these past few weeks. Why don't we quit being such glory hogs and spread a little of the action around? I mean, I'm not *that* selfish. . .'

Hannibal grinned. 'I am. . .'

TWENTY-EIGHT

The upper floors of the Lung Chin headquarters constituted a veritable labyrinth of separate rooms, each one assigned to a different purpose. Some rooms served as quarters for live-in bodyguards and hired helps; others were set up as offices from which numerous activities were directed by the organization's hierarchy. Any connoisseur of the Seven Capital Sins would have had no trouble finding a room that offered the corruption of his choice. As the more youthful members of the Lung Chin were fond of pointing out, this was the Disneyland of organized crime in Chinatown.

Sam and Sun Yeng were bound to chairs in a conference room filled with maps of the city, county, and state. Any unsuspecting soul might have looked over the maps and concluded that they were partitioned off in terms of local zoning ordinances. In fact, however, the charts detailed various slices of crime factions that operated the bulk of illicit activities throughout most of California. It was the hope of the Lung Chin that, with the newly-formed alliance with Chris Thomas and the recent blows dealt to Tommy Angel and Crazy Tommy Tillis, a greater slice of that criminal pie would end up being controlled by the Chinatown syndicate.

'We're going to die, aren't we, father?' Sun Yeng whispered, her voice cracked with emotion. She and Sam were tied with their backs to one another, so that even when she craned her neck as much as she could, she still could not see her father's face.

'We all die sometime,' Sam philosophized. He was sitting stoically in his chair, having answered Sun's question in his mind some time ago. He didn't feel sorrow for his position so much as for that of his daughter, who had not had the chance to live a full life. As a wave of grief for her fate suddenly washed over him, he clenched his teeth and said, 'I should have sent you away. . . with Tommy Chen and his family. Then you would be safe.'

'I'm glad that I'm here with you, father,' Sun said bravely. They fell silent and she struggled briefly against the firmness of her bonds. Her ankles and wrists were already on the verge of bleeding from her previous attempts at escaping. When she heard the rattling of the doorknob, she stopped what she was doing and sat upright, drawing in a deep breath. If her father could show courage and strength in the face of adversity, then so could she.

It was Stan Ling who opened the door and stepped into the room, followed by the elder Wan Chu. The two criminals were in high spirits, filled with the sense of gloating that comes when one has achieved a coveted prize, no matter the cost or inconvenience to others. Wan Chu hovered in front of Sam and shook his head at the restauranteur. The expression of pity on the old man's face was as transparent as the wax he routinely applied to his thin goatee.

'You have been extremely childish with us, Mr Yeng,' he told Sam. 'All we wanted was a little. Your behaviour has forced us to take everything.'

Sam stared at Wan Chu. 'You kill me, but let my daughter go,' he bargained. 'This not her affair.'

'You are mistaken, Mr Yeng,' Wan Chu countered. 'This is very much her affair. In fact, it is more than a mere affair. It is my understanding she was to be wed, and to show that I am not an unkind man, I have brought her a husband to share her last few moments with.'

Stan Ling disappeared in the hallway a moment, then

dragged Tommy Chen into the room. Sun's fiancé was bound by the hands and he was bruised wherever Sun Yeng could see.

'Tommy!' she gasped.

Tommy blinked and tried to focus on Sun as he was unceremoniously dumped into another chair and shoved near to the Yengs. He finally got a clear image of his beloved, and despite his battered condition, he managed the hint of a smile. 'I thought I would die before I had the chance to see you again.'

'Oh, Tommy, what have they done to you?'

'Be cautious with your loyalty to him, Sun Yen,' Wan Chu advised. 'He has sold the Lung Chin out already.'

'And I would do it again!' Tommy declared boldly. 'I just wish I could have done it sooner and done a better job of it!'

Stan Ling took a long step toward Tommy and cuffed the prisoner across the side of the face with the back of his hand. Chen's head jerked sharply to one side, then dropped forward listlessly. Ling grabbed him by the hair and tilted his face up so that Wan Chu could look at him.

'We should never have offered you the chance to join the Lung Chin,' Wan Chu told Tommy. 'But we correct our mistakes.'

'The only place you'll ever correct your mistakes is behind bars!' Tommy managed to sputter before he was struck again.

While Stan Ling was tying Chen to the chair, Wan Chu moved away and told the prisoners, 'As soon as your other friends arrive to try and get you out, our soldiers will trap them. . . and shortly afterwards we will be rid of all of you. For now, though, you may enjoy yourselves and catch up on old times, as the Americans say. There will be no new times for you. . .'

Stan Ling settled his gargantuan frame into a large swivel chair and propped his feet on the ledge. 'I'll keep and eye on them, Wan Chu. You go ahead and meet with Mr Thomas.'

Wan Chu bowed slightly, then left the room. He

shuffled down the corridor, then paused before an open room and glanced in. A hard-looking woman in a red outfit was leaning over a desk filled with loose papers, printing supplies, and a laminating machine.

'Is it ready yet?' Wan Chu asked. 'I cannot keep him waiting much longer.'

'Yes, Wan Chu.' The woman dropped a couple more items into a bulging manilla envelope, then brought it out to her leader. 'Forgive the delay, but I wanted to make sure everything was in proper order.'

Wan Chu clutched the envelope and continued down the corridor to the last room on the left. He opened the door and stepped into a plush chamber filled with exotic sculpture and padded divans. Chris Thomas was pacing irritably across the pile carpet, and when he spotted Wan Chu he anchored himself and clamped his hands against his hips as he demanded, 'I'd like to know what the hell I've been waiting for! You should have had me out of town and on my way to meet my wife by now! If I'd have known how incompetent the Lung Chin were –'

'We were concerned for your safety,' Wan Chu interrupted. 'Trust me, Mr Thomas. We are very capable, and the problems you had at the docks will not be repeated. The people responsible for the situation are being tended to.'

'You should have made sure they were taken care of *before* they started causing trouble!' Thomas accused, pointing his finger at Wan Chu. 'That's the way I would have done it. But to hell with that for now. You've got a contract to fulfil if you want your piece of my action.'

'Yes, and I believe this should cover it.' Wan Chu handed the envelope to Thomas and watched on as the other man opened it and checked the contents inside. 'You'll find a driver's licence, credit cards. . . everything you could possibly want to start a new life.'

' "Henry Enghard"?' Thomas read the name on the driver's licence. 'My name's gonna be Henry Enghard? What the hell kind of name is that? Sounds like a brand of beer.'

'It is a name that will serve you well,' Wan Chu said. 'We have run great risks to secure this identity for you and to smuggle you back to your former domain. It is unsafe for us to have you here. Our men who were captured at the boat know where we are.'

'And if they rat, the cops will be crawling around here like cockroaches,' Thomas realized. 'Great, just great!'

'If the police come,' Wan Chu explained, 'they will have much backing, you can be sure. We will have no choice but to let them enter. You must not be here when that happens.'

'Hey, I'm not the one who's holding things up around here,' Thomas reminded the Chinese chieftain. 'I've been ready to go since I got here.'

Wan Chu stepped to one side and motioned to the hallway. 'Then let us go. I will see that you are driven to your new address.'

Thomas shook his head violently. 'No way. You give me the keys to the car and a map of where I'm supposed to go, then I'll handle the rest on my own.'

'But Mr Thomas. . .'

'My name is Enghard, remember?' Thomas said hotly. 'Look, I want to leave this place on my own because the bottom line is I don't trust anybody but myself. How do I know you're not setting me up? After all, you have a lot to gain by trying to rub me out and lay claim to my turf.'

Wan Chu sighed, 'We are allies, Mr. . . Enghard. We must learn to work together. What if I were to accompany you, alone, to your new accommodation? You will have my constant presence as an assurance that there is nothing amiss, and we can take advantage of the time to get to know each other. We have many plans to discuss, after all.'

Thomas thought it through quickly, then grabbed his homburg from the divan closest to the door and pulled it down tight around his head. 'Okay, let's go for it!'

'After you, Mr Enghard.'

'No way, Wan Chu,' Thomas said. 'You go first. I always want you where I can see you.'

Wan Chu smiled wryly as he moved back out into the corridor. He murmured to himself, 'This is going to be a most intriguing alliance.'

'What'd you say?'

'Nothing,' Wan Chu replied. 'Nothing at all. . .'

As the two men proceeded down the hallway, they passed by the room where Tommy Chen and the Yengs were being held captive. Wan Chu signalled for Thomas to wait a moment, then he told Stan Ling, 'Have someone take your place here. I want you to be downstairs, to watch over things while I go for a ride with our friend here. I will call you when we reach his new home and you can send a car out to pick me up.'

'What about these three?' Stan Ling glanced over at the prisoners.

'After I am gone, have them killed. . .'

TWENTY-NINE

Wan Chu's cherry-red stretch limo was pulling up the incline leading to the street when a lone police cruiser sped around the corner and bore down on it.

'Hold on, 'cause it's bumber car time!' B.A. warned his cohorts as he slammed on the brakes and veered sideways. He'd timed the manoeuvre perfectly, and the patrol car butted side-to-side with the limo like a drunkard dancing the rumba. Neither car was severely damaged, but when they came to a rest after collision, they were straddling the driveway sideways.

The A-Team had been more prepared for what happened, and they were out of the cruiser even before it had stopped skidding. Rifles in hand, they hurried to the exposed doors of the limo, intercepting Wan Chu and Chris Thomas as they tried to stagger away from the vehicle.

'Well, well, who do we have here? Hannibal said as he grabbed Wan Chu by the arm. 'Looks to me like we just got ourselves the two birds in the bush.'

'Sorry about your limo, Wan Chu,' Peck said, 'but you'll have plenty of things to do while it's in the shop. If you're lucky, maybe you'll even have a chance to stamp a new set of licence plates for it.'

'I think you are mistaken,' Wan Chu said calmly. 'You do not have the upper hand here. We do.'

'Let's hear you say that once we get you away from your

home court advantage.' Hannibal guided Wan Chu around the front of the limo while B.A. and Murdock escorted Thomas, who was livid, shaking with rage.

'Damn you, Wan Chu!' he roared. 'You were supposed to give me protection! Hell, I use deoderant that does a better job that you!'

'Patience, Mr Enghard,' said Wan Chu. 'The tide is about to turn.'

Although Wan Chu had told Thomas they would be travelling alone to Thomas's new digs, he's been speaking only in terms of riders in the limousine. Arrangements had already been made for a motorcade of four sedans to flank the limo on its trip, and when the limo didn't round the corner on schedule, the four cars suddenly roared down the side street toward the scene of the crash. At the same time, Stan Ling led a handful of gunmen charging out of the basement garage.

'Freeze!' Ling ordered the A-Team.

'That's the second time we've heard that line tonight,' Peck muttered. 'You'd think it was winter already.'

B.A. inspected the two vehicles as Hannibal was getting ready to shove Wan Chu into the police cruiser. 'Forget it, Hannibal!' he called out. 'The cop car's stuck to the limo, man. It ain't goin' nowhere!'

'I was afraid you were going to say that, B.A.,' Hannibal said. He ducked a bullet that caromed off the roof of the car a few inches away from him, then tightened his grip on Wan Chu and started across the street, shouting over his shoulder at the others, 'Let's try that building with the glass door!'

As the A-Team dragged their captives out into the street, exposing themselves to the glow of the overhead lights, Murdock and Peck sprayed a ring of gunfire in all directions to keep any foolhardy Lung Chin sharpshooter from having a chance to concentrate on trying to pick off his boss's abductors without hitting Wan Chu or Thomas. Hannibal aimed his AR-15 at the doorway he'd mentioned and cut loose with a full clip. The glass panel in the door frame shattered, setting off a burglar alarm and leaving a large enough opening for the A-Team to squeeze through without cutting themselves. Wan Chu and Thomas both tried to shake free from their captors, but were unable to.

It was dark inside the building, with only the faintest flow from the outside streetlights trickling through the black gloom. The burglar alarm rang incessantly until Murdock spotted the small red bulb indicating its position and promptly shot it out with the last burst of his pistol. In the wake of sudden silence, the A-Team could hear Lung Chin gunmen rushing across the street in pursuit.

'Down this hallway!' Hannibal hissed, leading his men and the two prisoners further into the building. At the end of the corridor, they ducked into a large, darkened storage room filled with stacked crates. 'I have to admit, this wasn't part of the plan,' Hannibal said, 'and neither was that part about trying to mate the squad car with the limo, B.A., if you know what I mean.'

'If we woulda put new tyres on my van and used that instead of the cop car, we'd be outta here already!' B.A. grumbled.'

'Look at it this way, B.A.,' Peck rationalized. 'At least this way you didn't have to get your wheels shot up again. Let's be thankful for small favours.'

As the group crouched behind a mound of the stacked crates, Thomas seethed, 'Who are you guys?!'

'We're your worst dreams come true, pal.' Hannibal pressed the tip of his gun against Thomas's throat and whispered, 'If you raise your voice again, you'll lose it.'

B.A. loomed over Wan Chu and demanded, 'Where's those folks you grabbed from the hotel, sucker?!'

'They're alive,' Wan Chu answered softly. 'Which is more than I will be able to say of you shortly.'

'You better hope they're alive,' B.A. snapped. 'If you hurt them, I'm gonna yank your Lung right outta your Chin, dig?'

'Shhhhhhh!' Hannibal sniffed the air as he cased out their surroundings. Reaching into one of the crates they were hiding behind, he pulled out a string of Chinese firecrackers. 'Guys, I think we just got dropped into popgun heaven.'

The men's eyes had become accustomed to the darkness, and they were able to see that they were hiding in the main warehouse of a fireworks factory.

'Gunpowder,' Peck mumbled. 'My favourite spice.'

Outside the chamber, the A-Team heard the sound of other men entering the building, shouting frantically in Chinese as they probed their way into the darkened maze of rooms and corridors.

'B.A., grab one of those boxes and take it with us,' Hannibal commanded as he dragged Wan Chu out from their place of hiding. 'Let's retreat a little further and hope we can find a way to balance the odds a little more in our favour.'

As they led their prisoners deeper into the warehouse, Murdock nudged a large bulge in the lower pocket of Thomas' overcoat and asked him, 'Say, is that the Maltese Cow or are you just glad to see me?'

'What?!' Thomas snorted contemptuously.

Peck told the drug baron, 'Whatever you do, don't tell him it's the stuff of dreams, or he'll never get cured.'

'What?!' Thomas repeated.

Just as they were about to reach the back wall of the warehouse, Hannibal spotted something out of the corner of his eye and paused long enough to investigate. He reached down and pulled a canvas tarp off a knee-high cannon mounted on wheels. 'I think we just found ourselves an ace in the hole, boys. Come on, B.A., give me a hand with this. Murdock, keep a close watch on Mutt and Jeff here. Face, try to track down a back exit and make sure we've got a clear run for it when the time comes.'

B.A. moved aside a few crates tomake enough room to swing the cannon around so that it was pointing in the direction of the main doorway. Hannibal pried the lid off one of the crates and started stuffing fireworks into the cannon.

'Hey, not too many, man!' B.A. warned. 'We don't wanna blow ourselves up!'

179

'What are you doing?' Wan Chu asked Hannibal while keeping his eyes trained on the gun Murdock held on him and Thomas.

'You've heard of Christmas in July, haven't you?' Hannibal said. 'Well, we thought we'd start a new tradition, the Fourth of July in October.'

'You will kill us all with your stupidity,' Wan Chu warned.

'Oh, you're a fan of the Big Bang theory, are you?' Hannibal tossed one last cherry bomb into the cannon, then moved behind B.A., putting an unlit cigar in his mouth. 'Me, I just like a lively party.'

'I don't know how this sucker works!' B.A. said. 'How am I supposed to fire it?'

'Allow me,' Hannibal said, taking B.A.'s place behind the weapon. 'I used to work one of these things at the state fair when I was a kid.'

Peck rejoined the group and reported, 'I guess the fire marshal hasn't been keeping up with his rounds around here. There's a good twenty crates blocking the back exit. Other than some of the windows, the only way out is the same way we came in.'

'So much for plans,' Hannibal said. 'Well, we're just going to have to wing it, guys, because we got company!'

The beams of several flashlights appeared in the doorway to the warehouse, and behind one of them was the unmistakable outline of Stan Ling. The A-Team crouched in place as the shafts of light ventured into the storage room and began sweeping towards them.

'Over here!' Wan Chu suddenly blurted out.

All at once, the three beams focused on where the A-Team was holding Wan Chu and Thomas captive.

'Say cheese!' Hannibal cried out, firing the cannon. Like breath from hell, a scathing torrent of explosive flame charged out of the cannon with a deafening roar. The launched fireworks fanned out in all directions as rockets burrowed their way into other crates, triggering still more explosions. The room lit up with a hundred colours as the thunderous chain of detonations blew out the windows and sent the Lung Chin fleeing from the warehouse in fervent terror.

'Let's try one of the windows,' Peck shouted, pointing to an opening ten feet up the nearest wall. Crates were stacked before the wall in such a way as to make a staircase, and the A-Team was able to scramble up them with minimal difficulty. There was no need to keep a gun trained on either Wan Chu or Thomas, since they weren't going anywhere except the same way as their captors. The warehouse continued to rock about them under the force of the explosions, and a few errant rockets charged past them, threatening to ignite the veritable powderkegs they were climbing on.

B.A. was the first one out, and he discovered that a ledge ran beneath the window and as far as the fire escape that led down to a deserted parking lot. This was on the opposite side of the building from where they entered, and none of the Lung Chin were about. B.A. could hear sirens filling the night air as fire engines and police cars converged on the main entrance of the building.

'I think the cops are gonna keep your flunkies busy,' Hannibal told Wan Chu as they climbed out onto the ledge and threaded their way to the fire escape.

Peck emerged next, followed by Chris Thomas. The gangster had lost his homburg in the shuffle, but he kept both hands on the parcel in his overcoat pocket as he climbed out onto the ledge. His eyes darted about fiendishly, and when they spotted a shed below where he was standing, he decided to make a run for it. Throwing himself from the ledge, he landed on the sloped roof of the shed and slid down to the pavement.

'He's all mine!' Murdock cried out. He scurried along the ledge away from the fire escape, then leapt into the air as if he thought he could fly. Gravity had other ideas, though, and he plummeted earthward. Thomas was just rising to his feet when Murdock landed on top of him and brought him back to the ground. The parcel he'd removed from his overcoat fell free, and this time the ceramic figurine broke into more pieces than Humpty Dumpty after the great fall. Thomas tried to shake Murdock off him, but Murdock kept him pinned to the asphalt as he whispered into the gangster's ear, 'You're down for the ten count, sugarfoot, and now you got a date at the Big House Up The River. You should have known you couldn't pull a caper over the eyes of Mack Murdock!'

Peck clambered down the fire escape and rushed over to assist Murdock. Glancing at the broken figurine, he spotted a small black object the size of a bottle cap lying amidst the shards. 'Hmmmm,' he murmured as he picked it up for closer inspection. 'Murdock, I think what we have here is the Maltese Microfilm'

'Hey, you guys are pretty good,' Thomas grunted under Murdock's weight. He reeked of desperation and cheap flattery all of a sudden. 'I could use you in my operation. It'd be worth a nice slice to you.'

'Nice try, Thomas, but we aren't for sale. . . at least not to your type.' Peck turned to Hannibal, who was coming over with Wan Chu held between him and B.A. 'Hey, Hannibal, have a look at this!'

Hannibal waited until his cigar was lit to look over the microfilm. 'Gee, I wonder what could be on this?' He speculated, 'Let's think this through. Here we've got a guy coming home from overseas to start up his old racket again. . . what does he need? Huh? A few names, maybe? A few old phone numbers? All those neat buddies of his out there who stick people in pencil sharpeners for a living. . . Whaddya say, Chris? Am I getting warm?'

Thomas didn't say anything. B.A. came over and told Murdock to get off the man so he could jerk him to his feet. 'What we gonna do with these suckers, Hannibal?'

Hannibal saw a large spool of cable next to the shed Thomas had jumped on and went over to retrieve it. 'Give me a hand, Face. I think we'll hog-tie our guests here and leave them for the cops when they get around to checking things out back here. I don't think we want to stick around for an interview, especially since we wrecked up one of their cars. If there's one thing a good cop hates, it's when somebody messes up one of their cars.'

B.A. and Peck hurriedly tied Wan Chu and Thomas together, then hauled the other end of the cable over to the fire escape. With some difficulty, they managed to haul the criminals up so that they were hanging upside down from the bottom of the fire escape grillwork.

'Kinda look like bats, don't they?' Hannibal said.

Murdock wasn't about to settle for so ordinary a description. Eyeing the prisoners, he said, 'They were just a matched set of sociopathic urges under a pair of bad haircuts. Their world had gone topsy-turvy, and by the time their ride was over, they'd be in bunks at Quentin, marking off days on the wall. . .'

'Okay, guys, let's get out of here,' Hannibal shouted over a renewed set of explosions sounding from within the warehouse. 'This isn't exactly safe for us, either.'

As the A-Team fled into the shadows of the nearest alley, Murdock intoned, 'But then, what was safe, I wondered? Life? That's rich. Set 'em up and tell me another one, buddy. You wanna know what's safe in this life? Sitting in church and eating fibre. The rest? Well, you just take your chances. . .'

'Let's get to the hospital and drop this fool off!' B.A. cried. 'I can't take his jive any more! If he doesn't shut up, I'm gonna give him a taste of my fist!'

'You must remember this,' Murdock sang, 'A fist is but a fist. . .'

And so it went on as they were swallowed by the night. . .

EPILOGUE

By the end of the week, the Golden Pagoda was still closed, but a hand-painted sign posted over the entrance promised that the restaurant's Grand Re-Opening would take place the following Monday. Inside, carpenters, electricians, and interior decorators worked around one another refurbishing the bar and dining room. The A-Team was there, taking it all in along with the Yengs and Tommy Chen. The rift between B.A. and Murdock had widened considerably over the past few days, and B.A. had reached the point where he refused to even acknowledge the presence of his greatest tormentor. He sat at his end of the table, arms folded across his massive chest as he watched the new mirror being installed behind the bar, paying no heed to the whimpering soul next to him.

'Awwwwwww, come on, B.A.,' Murdock pleaded, wringing his hands. 'How many times do I gotta tell ya? I don't need to go back to the vets. Everything's worked itself out and I'm off the Mack Murdock kick for good! I just know it this time, B.A., you gotta believe me. It was just a phase I was going through. You remember? Like that time I thought I was a plaid jacket named Willy.'

'I remember that,' Peck cracked from across the table, winking at Sam and Sun Yeng.

'Yeah,' Hannibal muttered, 'He kept wanting everybody to wear him. . .'

When Murdock fell to his knees and inched closer into

B.A.'s field of vision, B.A. turned to the others. 'Tell him to forget it, Hannibal! When B.A. Baracus makes up his mind, it stays made.'

'Oh, B.A., you don't mean that now,' Murdock scoffed, changing tack. He reached out to put an arm around B.A.'s shoulder, but decided B.A. might yank it out of its socket and pulled it back. 'Just think if all the *fun* you and me have always had. I mean, darn it all anyway, we're. . . we're soul-mates, that's what we are, B.A., soul-mates.'

'Man's lookin' for serious bodily harm' B.A. warned. 'Somebody better tell him to move outta my punchin' range before I decide I gotta stretch my arms all of a sudden.'

Murdock stood up and walked away from the table, covering his eyes with the back of his hand and otherwise indulging himself in melodramatics. 'Cruel fate! I am this man's absolutely most devoted friend. . . I am as loyal to him as a dog is to its master, and yet, for all –'

'Now he's turnin' into a dog again!' B.A. got up from his seat and headed for the front door. 'I'm goin' to put more money in the meter. Air's thick with Murdock's jive. I can hardly breathe.'

'B.A., buddy. . .' Murdock followed Baracus out of the restaurant, leaving the others without entertainment. There was a moment of awkward silence, punctuated by the hammering of a carpenter, then Sam Yen cleared his throat to draw their attention.

'Everything turning out okay thanks to A-Team,' he said. 'Restaurant open soon, with no Lung Chin to come for money. Happy day for Sam Yeng. Very happy day.'

'We're glad to see it happen, Sam,' Hannibal said.

'Just like we'll be glad to see those profit shares coming in again?' Peck asked.

'No, I'll be even more glad to see those.' Hannibal turned to Sun and Tommy Chen, who were sitting next to one another, their eyes filled with a shy yearning. 'How about you two? Things a little better now between you?'

'Much,' Sun replied. She took Tommy's hand and held

it tightly. 'We're sort of getting back together.'

Tommy smiled and divulged, 'She's thinking it over but I want her to be my wife. I never stopped loving her, even when. . .'

His voice trailed off. Sun kissed him lightly on the cheek and told him, 'That's behind us now, Tommy. We don't have to even think about it.'

'I be right back,' Sam Yeng said as he rose from his chair and headed off into the kitchen.

'I appreciate what you guys did,' Tommy told Hannibal and Peck. 'I'm not sure I'd have handled things right without you forcing me to have some guts.'

'You already had the guts, Tommy,' Hannibal said, 'And you didn't need any of our help in overpowering that guard and helping Sam and Sun to escape the Lung Chin headquarters that night we had our hands full with Wan Chu and that Thomas guy. Face it, kid, you've got hero written all over you.'

'Speak of heroes!' Sam called out from the kitchen. He parted the swinging doors and emerged with two huge platters containing servings of Peking duck. His daughter came over to help him with the offerings, and both Hannibal and Peck began to salivate as they stared at the plates set before them. Sam boasted, 'This is meal fit for heroes like my friends in A-Team! Enjoy!'

'I'm sure we will,' Hannibal said as he unfolded a napkin and set it across his lap. 'After two other botched efforts, it's great to finally have a chance to dig into one of these.'

B.A. came back inside, with Murdock still at his side like an eel hoping to latch onto a shark. B.A. kept shoving him away, but Murdock bounced back as if he were connected to B.A. by springs. 'Pretty please with sugar on it? Sugar and cherries on top?'

'Forget it, Murdock!' B.A. said as he sat back down at the table.

'Pretty please with sugar, cherries, whipped cream and those little bitty oranges you cut up and make flowers out of like that on top. . . and maybe some meatballs?'

B.A. reached out and grabbed Murdock by the lapels of his flight jacket, then brought the aviator's face to within a few inches of his own. 'All right! You got it, sucker!'

When B.A. let go of him, Murdock staggered a few steps backwards as if he'd just taken an uppercut to the chin. He stared at B.A., incredulous. 'What?'

'I said all right!' B.A. picked up his knife and fork and hovered both utensils over his meal as he glared at Murdock. 'You want talk?' I'll talk with you, long as the first thing you do is shut up!'

As B.A. started carving his duck and chewing the first few bites, Murdock swooned. 'Did you hear that?' he asked Hannibal and Peck. 'He's my friend again. My bud, my compad, my charming amigo. . .'

Murdock tried to give B.A. a hug. Baracus exploded, bolting from his chair and hefting Murdock off his feet. 'You sick fool, Murdock! You do all this stuff just to drive me crazy, don't you? He pinned his nemesis against the wall. 'Well, I'm sick of it, sucker! I'm sick of hearing your crazy rap! I'm gonna pop your lid and pour you out.'

Murdock squirmed pathetically in B.A.'s grasp, trying to fight off the ghost of Philip Marlowe that seemed intent on overcoming him. 'It finally hit me like a ton of Teddy bears,' he finally droned out of the side of his mouth. 'I wanted my Mommy.'

Peck and Hannibal traded glances. Peck said, 'You know, Hannibal, maybe B.A.'s right. It might be time we got Murdock back to his ink blots.'

'I'm not going anywhere until I finish eating,' Hannibal declared.

Tommy Chen finished a mouthful of duck, then asked the A-Team, 'So, now that things are calming down here, what are your plans?'

'Oh, we'll just wait and see what comes together,' Hannibal said.

'I don't understand,' Tommy said.

'I think what Hannibal's trying to say,' Peck explained, 'is that he loves it when a plan comes together. . .'

187